It was a

Candace knew it from the minute she saw him. Clint was tall and tanned and lean and—the small tinglings of attraction she'd felt the other day hit her this day like a live electric current.

Last week she'd been tired and preoccupied.

This day, he struck her as, quite possibly, the most attractive man she'd ever seen. Now that they shared the problem of her son, now that they were no longer attorney and client, Candace was startled to feel impulses awaken which had been forced into a long slumber.

"Good morning," he said, and the sound of his voice, whisky-rough, rubbed over her newly sensitized nerve endings like velvet.

"Hello," she managed, and wondered why her senses were so suddenly running amok.

Dear Reader,

It's May—spring gardens are in full bloom, and in the spirit of the season, we've gathered a special "bouquet" of Silhouette Romance novels for you this month.

Whatever the season, Silhouette Romance novels *always* capture the magic of love with compelling stories that will make you laugh and cry; stories that will move you with the wonder of romance, time and again.

This month, we continue our FABULOUS FATHERS series with Melodie Adams's heartwarming novel, *What About Charlie?* Clint Blackwell might be the local hero when it comes to handling troubled boys, but he never met a rascal like six-year-old Charlie Whitney. And he never met a woman like Charlie's lovely mother, Candace, who stirs up trouble of a different kind in the rugged cowboy's heart.

With drama and emotion, Moyra Tarling takes us to the darker side of love in *Just a Memory Away.* After a serious accident, Alison Montgomery is unable to remember her past. She struggles to learn the truth about her handsome husband, Nick, and a secret about their marriage that might be better left forgotten.

There's a passionate battle of wills brewing in Joleen Daniels's *Inheritance.* The way Jude Emory sees it, beautiful Margret Brolin has stolen the land and inheritance that is rightfully his. How could a man as proud as Jude let her steal his heart as well?

Please join us in welcoming new author Lauryn Chandler who debuts this month with a lighthearted love story, *Mr. Wright.* We're also proud to present *Can't Buy Me Love* by Joan Smith and *Wrangler* by Dorsey Kelley.

In the months to come, watch for books by more of your favorites—Diana Palmer, Suzanne Carey, Elizabeth August, Marie Ferrarella and many more. At Silhouette, we're dedicated to bringing you the love stories you love to read. Our authors and editors want to hear from you. Please write to us; we take our reader comments to heart.

Happy reading!

Anne Canadeo
Senior Editor

WHAT ABOUT CHARLIE?

Melodie Adams

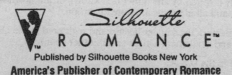

Silhouette
R O M A N C E™
Published by Silhouette Books New York
America's Publisher of Contemporary Romance

For Jake, Jonathan and Alex, the three musketeers.
Love you guys. You make the world go round.

SILHOUETTE BOOKS
300 East 42nd St., New York, N.Y. 10017

WHAT ABOUT CHARLIE?

ISBN: 0-373-08934-1

First Silhouette Books printing May 1993

Books by Melodie Adams

Silhouette Romance

I'll Fly the Flags #265
A Dangerous Proposition #516
The Medicine Man #647
In the Family Way #722
What About Charlie? #934

Silhouette Special Edition

Gentle Possession #152

MELODIE ADAMS

spent her childhood years in various states west of the Mississippi and claims that it was "a terrific, ever-changing, always interesting way to grow up." Still, in spite of all the wonderful places she's seen, Melodie's favorite way to relax is to spend the day in the sun, a tall glass of ice tea in one hand and a good romance in the other.

Clint Blackwell on Fatherhood:

Well, I did it. Made it through this spring and summer, and now the three of us together are an accomplished fact—or, as Charlie would be quick to tell me, a fait accompli. I'm a husband . . . and a father.

The hick rancher and the snotty city wonder-boy—who'd have thought we'd make such a team? I've never met a kid like Charlie. If I can keep a half step ahead of him and that computer over the next twenty years, I'll be doing better than good.

Charlie and I are different—*really* different—but differences make the world go round. My world has been going around pretty well ever since I first met Charlie and his mom. I love that kid, and I want to let him know, deep down in his gut, that whatever snag and differences we hit, we'll always work them through. Always. I swear.

Chapter One

Beeeep... "Candace, hi, it's Jack. Listen, I'm going to need you to run some contracts out to the Blackwell ranch this afternoon. I'd planned to go myself, but I'm going to be tied up with a new client. Call me when you get in. Oh, and the school called. Your kid's disappeared again...."

"...Hello, Mrs. Whitney. This is Peter Drake from school. It's now 12:55, and we cannot locate Charles. Please call the minute you get home...."

"...Mrs. Whitney, Peter Drake again. It's 2:15 and your son has returned. Seems he...went out to lunch, and...needed to stop at the bank. Mrs. Whitney, we need to talk. Immediately." Beeeep!

The machine clicked off, then whirred as it rewound.

Candace closed her eyes and leaned her forehead against one of the metal bookcases that flanked the desk she'd set up at one end of her living room. They had three desks in this tiny rented two-bedroom house. One here, old and oak and scuffed and very utilitarian, which held her business things and related files. One in her small bedroom, an antique cherrywood writing desk, for personal business and correspondence. And one, an L-shaped pressboard thing in Charles's room, which took up a large corner and held his computer and printer.

Charles was six years old.

Candace stood up, flexed her tight shoulder muscles and wondered what business he'd had at the bank.

"This just can't go on," Peter Drake said at three o'clock that afternoon. He removed his black-framed glasses and pinched the bridge of his nose. He wasn't an old man by any means—maybe forty-four or -five. Yet, looking at the frustrated elementary school principal, Candace had the feeling that coping with Charles was aging the man daily.

"I'm sorry, Mr. Drake," she said, knowing how he felt. But what did you do with a child whose precociousness and intelligence refused to submit to rules and regulations? Charles wasn't a bad kid. He was just...unmanageable.

"First-graders," Peter Drake said, eyeing her from across his desk, "do not leave school grounds because they feel like 'going out to lunch.' Nor do they meander off to the First National Savings and Loan to 'take care of some business.' First-graders, Mrs. Whitney, do not *have* business at banks. They don't have *business* anywhere!''

Candace lowered her eyes, wanting to give the principal a few seconds to compose himself. In the two months that Charles had been in school here, Candace and Drake had met half a dozen times. He didn't understand her son, and Candace didn't blame him for that.

Although the Progressive Center of Learning out in LA, which Charles had attended year-round since age three, had, as promised, "nurtured and celebrated the child's individuality," and it had "sought, found and encouraged the child's unique interests and special brilliance," it had not, in any way, prepared her son for life outside of the center's esteemed and very expensive walls.

For three years Candace had received glowing evaluations and enthusiastic reports of her son's progress.

So she had been shocked when, upon moving back to Missouri, the public Elm Street Elementary School had deemed, and perhaps even proven, that Charles Eric Whitney was virtually dysfunctional.

"He says he has a savings account at First National," Peter Drake said, calmer now, but no less frustrated and bewildered.

"He does," Candace murmured. "His father opened one for him when he was born. When we moved here, we transferred the funds—"

"And a stock portfolio."

"Just a...small one. You know his father's a stockbroker," Candace said, feeling like she was on trial—and guilty. In the past few months she'd realized that many of her life's decisions had been wrong. But they'd seemed so...progressive, so state-of-the-art, so...*right* at the time.

She wasn't an unintelligent human being. She'd graduated twentieth in her class at SMSU, then been in the top ten percentile in law school. Out in LA she'd had no trouble securing a job and had risen quickly and steadily as a corporate lawyer within the prestigious firm of Ryner, Ryner, Jarrell and Collingsworth.

Between herself and Eric, they'd brought in over two hundred thousand dollars a year by their seventh year of marriage. He drove a Jaguar, she a BMW, and they'd bought a house outside the city because it seemed a good place to raise their son. They'd taken an active interest in their son's environment and education and enrolled him in the most expensive, most modern, most nurturing school they could find.

Yet...

What was it they said about best-laid plans? And the paving material for the road to hell?

Looking back, all Candace could see was a mountain of mistakes. Looking ahead, what she could see was a lot of undoing that needed to be done. Somehow. Some way. A breakthrough was near, Candace was sure. All they had to do was find a way to penetrate Charles's tough little armor.

Peter Drake leaned back in his chair and stared at the acoustical tile on the ceiling.

"I'm not a man who runs away from a challenge, Mrs. Whitney," he said, then looked over at her. "In fact, I love a challenge. I love kids. That's why I got into this profession. But I really have to tell you that I'm at a loss here—and so is Mrs. Dale. I hoped that when we moved Charles into her class last month, things would change. She's one of our best teachers, Mrs. Whitney. Frieda Dale is one of the most caring, giving, concerned teachers on our staff. She keeps up with new information and studies and research on child development. She attends advanced courses every summer. She—"

"I know," Candace said. "She's a wonderful woman. Look, Mr. Drake, I know it's been hard. Believe me, I know. But if we could just . . . work with Charles a little longer. He's only been in public school for two months. The structure, the rules, the curriculum—it's all quite an adjustment to make. Between that and the move and the divorce and everything, it's been hard for him. Hard for both of us."

"I appreciate that, Mrs. Whitney."

"Candace," she said. "Call me Candace." It seemed suddenly ridiculous to continue the formality when conversations with this man were obviously going to be a very regular part of her life.

"Candace, then," said Drake, putting on his glasses and giving her the look of a man coming to a decision. "Candace. As I said, I appreciate that it's been difficult for both you and Charles."

"But?" Candace said, wary now.

"But..." He sighed and threw up his hands. "The fact is that if the boy doesn't change, I'll have no choice but to..."

"To what?" Candace asked.

He shook his head. "I can't believe I'm about to say this.... Mrs. Whitney, I've been an educator for more than twenty years, and never in my experience have I even heard of a first-grader being..."

"Being..."

"Well, being asked to find education...elsewhere."

"You mean," Candace said, rising in anger, "being expelled."

"I don't know what else to do," Drake said, also rising, and through her anger Candace felt sorry for him. He didn't *want* to do this, she knew. In fact, it was the last thing he wanted to do. If things didn't change and Peter Drake had to resort to expulsion of a first-grader, it would mean a major failure to the man as an educator.

It didn't say much for the woman as a mother, either.

Or for Charles as a little boy.

That was the worst of it, what had been made of Charles. It wasn't his fault, but if she didn't change things—change *him*—the world would never see the wonderful little boy inside. They'd only see the three-and-a-half-foot-tall incorrigible tyrant that had unintentionally been created.

"I understand your position, Mr. Drake," she said, hooking the strap of her bag over her shoulder. "But I don't think it will come to that. Things around the Whitney household are going to change, starting today. I'll go get my son now and take him home."

He walked her to his office door. "I hope they do change, Mrs. Whitney—Candace. Charles could be such a delight, a real asset to our school. If we could just..."

"I know," Candace said grimly. "If you could just get some control."

He nodded, giving a halfhearted smile. "I hope you understand."

"Unfortunately, Mr. Drake, I do."

Candace left with the principal's beaten look burning an image into her brain. Enough was enough. She was an adult. She was the boy's mother. There was no reason on God's green earth that she could not gain authority and control over a six-year-old boy.

She found him at the back of Frieda Dale's classroom. It was three-thirty now, and the other students had left to go home.

Frieda Dale, a trim fortyish brunette, greeted Candace with a smile that held sympathy and more—a smile that too closely matched the one Peter Drake had offered. A smile that said, *Good luck, kid, but we've done all we can. You're on your own.*

"Charles," Candace said, heels clicking as she crossed the room.

Charles didn't look up or turn around to face her. He stood, unmoving, back to her, blond head bent, face near the small cage that held a rodent of some kind.

"Look at this, Mom," Charles said. "I think we should call the humane society."

Candace paused and fought the urge to rub her pounding temples. "Charles," she said firmly, "let's go."

He turned then, looked at her, shrugged, as if he could find no reason for her attitude but would humor her, as was his lot in life.

"Say goodbye to Mrs. Dale," Candace said.

"Goodbye, Mrs. Dale." His voice was small and sweet and obedient. Not sullen, angry, resentful. Not worried in the least that he had left school grounds again and knew he'd be in trouble.

That was the thing. When punishment didn't faze a child, where was your leverage? It was easy enough for teachers and principals and other parents to suggest that Charles needed more discipline. Easy enough to suggest spankings, withholding of privileges, parental disapproval. Easy enough to suggest anything. Except with Charles, it didn't work.

He accepted punishment as his due, in a very calm, logical, adultlike manner. If he'd done the crime, he'd do the time. And then go off and leave school the very next day if he felt he had a valid reason.

"Get your bike," Candace said out in the parking lot.

It was early April but felt like late May. They'd had a mild winter and promise of a gorgeous spring. The air smelled wet and new and earthy and reminded Candace of her years growing up here, long lazy summers, crisp, snowy winters.

She'd wanted that for Charles, too. Yet, California-born, he wasn't impressed with either the climate or the lifestyle of small-town midwestern living.

She opened the trunk, waiting for Charles to put his bicycle inside.

"I can just ride it home," Charles said.

"In the trunk," Candace said. "You're not going to be riding it for a while."

He frowned slightly but didn't protest. He wheeled the bike over to her and she lifted it, careful not to let it touch her clothes—rust ultrasuede pants and a cream silk blouse. Her workday wasn't over yet. She'd spent the morning at the courthouse, and now had to run the contracts out to the Blackwell ranch. Candace hoped going over them with the rancher wouldn't take long. She and Charles had some heavy talking to do tonight.

Closing the trunk, she slid behind the wheel.

"Buckle up," Charles said, already fastened in his own seat belt.

Candace did and headed for the old graveyard highway, the potholed two-lane that would take them to the Blackwell ranch.

"Hey, Mom," Charles said, as they passed first the veteran's cemetery and then the Cedar Grove Baptist church with its old cemetery out back. "You know why they put fences around graveyards?"

She looked at him, steeling herself against the humor in the blue eyes that looked even larger behind his gold-rimmed, aviator-style glasses. He was in trouble, she reminded herself. He should be feeling the threat of discipline right now. Feeling the sting of her silence and disapproval.

"They put fences around graveyards," Charles said, "because everybody's dying to get in."

Candace took a deep breath, wishing she could just ignore what had happened today and what was going to happen in the future if things didn't change. All she wanted was for Charles to be happy, normal, to fit in and to have friends. As it was, the children at Elm Street school avoided and shunned Charles.

He was too different, Candace knew. The other children were just learning to read things like "run spot run" and "Dick, see spot run," and Charles had been following the stock market in the morning paper for over a year. No, Candace realized again, she and Eric had not done the boy any favors.

"Charles, why did you leave school today?" She watched the road, but knew it was a straight shot out to the Blackwell place. Eight miles out on old graveyard road, then left on the ranch's long drive.

Her side vision saw Charles look out the passenger window.

"We were having fish sticks for lunch," he said. "I hate fish sticks."

"You could have taken a lunch," Candace said. "We have the school menu at home, and you could have checked it this morning and taken your lunch."

"That probably would have been better," Charles said. "Next time I should do that."

Candace sighed. No defense. No tantrums. No arguments to her obvious logic. Yet her son was honest, even in his apparent acquiescence. She was very aware, and knew he was, too, of his choice of words. Not, I *will* do that, but I *should* do that. A world of difference between those two little words.

"And the bank?" she said. "Charles, what were you doing today at the bank?"

"Checking on my money," he said. "S & Ls are in a lot of trouble right now. I'm going to switch my account over to a regular bank. I called that one on Main Street. They're paying six and a half percent on savings."

Candace felt her temples pound.

"Tonight," she said, "you and I are going to sit down and have a long talk. Things are going to have to change, Charles. Mr. Drake says that if you keep on like this, he'll have no choice but to...expel you from school. He doesn't want to have to do that, Charles. He likes you and thinks you're a fine boy. But the school has rules. You have to learn to follow them."

He used his forefinger to push the glasses up on the bridge of his little-boy nose. He gave her a long, empty look that tugged at her heart and made her want to take her stern words back. Maybe they were necessary to get through, and maybe the situation really was getting serious, but he was just a little boy, and he had been through a lot.

She reached out, put a hand on his stiff shoulder, stroking his silky blond hair. "People are dying to get in, huh?" she said. "That sounds like *my* brand of cornball joke."

She wished for a smile, but didn't get one. Sobriety and silence were their companions the rest of the way out to the ranch.

"Hey, Clint!" someone shouted. "Think fast!"

He thought fast, saw the egg coming and cupped his hands to catch it—but not fast enough. The egg hit him flat on the chest, shell cracking, ooze splattering.

Clint Blackwell scowled. "That's really good, you guys. Really mature." As he spoke, his gaze flashed around the dimness of Alice's henhouse, looking for the culprit. The four teenage boys cackled, any or all as guilty as the next.

So Clint thought fast. The pile of eggs they'd gathered for Alice sat in the basket, a regular arsenal. Clint grabbed the basket, took two eggs in one hand and began firing. Ray, Bobby, Ian and Dean yelped and ran.

He chased them out of the gloom and into daylight, firing steadily. Egg bombs sailed, hit and splattered, catching Ray on the back of the head, Bobby between the shoulders and Dean smack in the middle of the seat of his jeans. Ian took shelter behind the big watering trough next to the holding corral.

Clint kept throwing. Bobby took an egg in the face, Ray a couple of slimy body shots and Dean one in the bare belly. Serves him right for going shirtless in April.

He ran out of eggs just as someone shouted, "Hey, no fair! Ian's the one that did it!"

And Ian, clean and goo-less, popped up from behind the trough. Grinning, triumphant, smug.

Clint chuckled, started around the corral toward the house. "Then I guess Ian can be the one to explain to Alice why she doesn't have any eggs. Here, Ian." He walked over, holding out the empty basket.

Ian got to his feet. "Aw, Clint, come on. Alice'll have my head."

"Or turn you over her knee."

He held out the basket.

Ian reluctantly reached to take it. "Come on, Clint—"

Clint grabbed the boy's wrist, then his back belt loop. In two seconds Ian Gladstone was off his feet. Clint dropped him cleanly into the watering trough.

"That's okay, Ian." He grinned. "I'll tell Alice for you."

Just for good measure he ducked the boy's dark head underwater one more time.

Spluttering, Ian howled. Bobby, Dean and Ray hooted and laughed and scraped goo off themselves.

Clint, grinning, swinging the basket by its handle, sauntered toward his house to change his shirt.

Then he paused halfway, squinting at the bronze BMW that had stopped up the drive—and at the tall, auburn-haired woman standing watching beside it.

Chapter Two

"Hello," he said easily. "Welcome to the festivities."

"Mr. Blackwell?" Candace said doubtfully.

The Blackwell name was and always had been prominent in Cedar Grove. While she'd never known a Blackwell personally, Candace remembered the name from way back. The Double C was the biggest cattle ranch in the area, with a reputation, too, for the quarter horses bred and raised on the land.

She looked at the man who had been throwing eggs at those boys and dunking one in the horse trough. He had tobacco-colored hair, a white, easy grin, dusty brown boots, and a worn chambray work shirt with a big round wet spot on the chest. And a basket dangling from the loop of thumb and forefinger.

"Clint Blackwell," he said and started to extend a hand. Having a second thought, he looked at the hand, saw the grime and flashed the grin again, wiping the hand on his work-dusty jeans.

Next to her Candace saw Charles prop his chin on the frame of the opened car window.

"I'm Candace Whitney," she said. "Jack Harden asked me to bring some contracts out. He said he'd call so you'd expect me?"

"Ah." Blackwell nodded. "Okay, great. I wasn't expecting you because I haven't been up to the house for a while, and my housekeeper's out, so I didn't get the message. Come on in, though. I'll clean up a little and we can get to it."

He moved a step closer and bent over to look in at Charles. "Who's this? Your boyfriend?"

Charles's eyebrows rose fractionally in surprise, and Candace smiled, warming to the friendly rancher. Easy, confident and open, he combined these qualities with a glint of ready humor in his gray eyes, a faint smile on a mouth that suggested a grin was one of his most-used expressions.

"This is my son," Candace said, "Charles Whitney. Charles, this is Mr. Blackwell."

"Clint," Blackwell said, still bent over to greet Charles at his eye level. "Just call me Clint. Glad to meet you, Charlie."

Charles gave Blackwell a long look, and Candace winced, knowing how he hated to be called Charlie. Eric's doing. Even when Charles was an infant, Eric had insisted on no baby names, no nonsense. Charles was a name with dignity; Chuck and Charlie weren't.

This minute, there was a haughty look in the tilt of Charles's chin. At six years old his dignity was affronted.

"Charles," Candace said, warning, "say hello to Mr. Blackwell."

"Sure, Charlie," Blackwell said. "Don't be shy. I don't throw *everybody* in the water trough."

Charles's stare was downright rude.

"Charles," Candace said, "say hello to Mr. Blackwell."

"Sure," Charles said, and smiled sweetly. "Hello, Clinty. It's nice to meet you, too."

"Charles!"

He blinked behind his glasses, all wide-eyed innocence. "What?"

Candace flashed an apologetic look at Clint Blackwell. "Would you excuse us for one second? Mother-son chat."

"No problem," Blackwell said, dropping back from the car, studying the ground and kicking at it absently with a dusty brown boot.

Yet Candace was conscious of him as, embarrassed and angry, she bent to the car window to chastise her son. "He said I could call him by his first name!"

"Well, he certainly didn't say you could call him Clinty!" Candace whispered back.

"I never said he could call me Charlie, either."

Sometimes whispers carried farther than normally voiced words. Clint grinned at the conversation and wandered farther off, out of earshot, while the woman dealt with her recalcitrant son.

So that was the problem, he thought. The boy didn't like to be called Charlie. A little tyke, barely school age, and already stiff and stuffy as a banker... or a lawyer. Or a lawyer's unfortunate son.

Not that Clint had anything against bankers or lawyers per se. And while he didn't believe you could judge the individual by the stereotype, his own experience had simply told him that they tended toward a stuffiness that always made him long to do something outrageous, liven them up.

Hey! Snap out of it! he always wanted to tell people who seemed too busy and preoccupied to enjoy life at all. He wanted to tell them what he'd had to learn, that life was a journey and not a destination. That if you focused too much on "someday" and "ultimate outcome," you missed the only really important thing—the days and minutes and quiet misty mornings that made up the trip.

But... that was his own philosophy, learned and earned the hard way. And everyone certainly had the right to his or her own opinion. Still, it always stuck in his craw to see a kid being expected—or even allowed—to be anything but what Clint believed to be a sovereign right—a plain, ordinary, snowball-throwing, mud-puddle-splashing, grass-stained, rainbow-awed, Santa Claus-believing kid. The way he saw it, you had one shot at childhood. And being born to dry, serious-minded parents shouldn't negate your rights to childhood's magic and silliness.

Charles, for Pete's sake. You saddle a tyke with a name like that, you established an image heavy with expectations. Charles was no name for a kid; it was a name a young man should be allowed to grow into.

"Mr. Blackwell?"

From behind him.

Ms. Candace Whitney was now standing with her son beside her next to the car, one hand holding a briefcase. The other resting rather firmly on the shoulder of Charles.

"I apologize for that little scene," Candace Whitney said. "It was very unprofessional, and I assure you it won't happen again."

"No problem," Clint said. "Kids'll be kids." Or they ought to be.

He cast a glance at Charles.

"So you don't like to be called Charlie, huh?"

"No," the boy said, and Clint saw his mother's fingers tighten on his shoulder in warning. "No, sir, Mr. Blackwell."

Clint gestured toward the house, and they began walking. "*Mister* Blackwell?" he said to the boy. "What happened to 'Clinty'? I sort of liked it. Nobody ever called me Clinty before."

The boy shot him an appraising look, and Clint grinned, knowing this would catch him off guard. Like Ian in the watering trough. Sometimes you could gain a lot of ground just by doing the unexpected, breaking the preconceived notions held by a child about adult reactions.

What had that school counselor told him last winter when they were talking about Ray? *You're nuts, Blackwell, but whatever you're doing, it works. Being out at the ranch has been better for Ray than therapy....*

Clint looked over toward the corral, thinking of his present charges. Bobby, Ray, Dean and Ian were lounging against the rail fence, staring shamelessly.

"Hey, you guys! Don't you have some work to do?"

They groaned and grimaced, but, Clint noted with satisfaction, they moved, each drifting off to finish the afternoon's chores. Not bad for a group who, six months ago, had been out of control and on the road to juvenile hall.

At first it had been tough with each of the boys and each of their rebellious styles. He'd started with Ray, and after seeing the progress, had taken on the others, one by one. Ian had been last, a particularly hard case to crack, but he, too, was coming right along.

Now Clint found himself looking forward to the boys' summer vacations, when they'd expressed an interest in working for him full-time. Bobby and Ray had even asked about maybe sleeping in the bunkhouse once in a while.

Clint, at this suggestion, had played tough and gruff, but the idea had touched him more than the little delinquents would ever know. As far as he was concerned, they could do more than sleep in the bunkhouse. They could just move themselves right into the main house and add a little noise and life to the old mausoleum.

But no. That would be getting too involved. Not good for the boys. Not fair to their parents. Probably not even good for him. Still, the idea of having a houseful of boisterous teenagers appealed.

By now he'd planned on having a bunch of kids of his own. But time had somehow gotten away from him and Meg, moving too fast. Always too much to do that year, too many big, important plans. But *next* year they'd start that family. And next year. And next.

And now Meg was gone and Clint was thirty-eight years old and alone.

Oh, yes, life was a journey.

But the goal, the big objective, was not to someday *arrive*. The goal, at least for Clint nowadays, was to seize each moment and milk it for all it was worth. And not lose any more of his life waiting for someday to live.

"So, Charles," Clint Blackwell said as he poured coffee into two stoneware mugs, "you ever been on a real ranch?"

"No," Charles said and took a drink of the lemonade Blackwell had seen to first. "You ever been to a real town?"

"Charles!" Candace could not believe her ears. After the talking-to she'd just given him out at the car, she would have expected, even from Charles, more restraint than this.

Instead of being insulted, as was Charles's intent, Clint Blackwell laughed. Heartily. "I'll say one thing for you, kid. You've got spirit."

"That he has," Candace said, cheeks hot. "Charles, we have some business to take care of. I suggest you eat your cookies, drink your lemonade and keep quiet. Understood?"

"All right," Charles said, taking a bite of a chocolate-chip cookie.

"If you'd like to watch some TV or something, you can take your snack into the living room," Blackwell said.

"All right." The picture of acquiescence, Charles stood up, picked up his plate and glass and followed Blackwell out of the big kitchen.

A minute later the rancher returned.

"I'm sorry," Candace murmured, taking the sheaf of contracts from her briefcase. "Charles isn't always so . . . insulting. We've just been having some problems lately. Thank you for being so gracious in spite of him."

"I like kids," Blackwell said, taking a chair at the end of the big pine table. "You've got yourself a sharp one there."

"Mmm," Candace murmured in agreement. "A little too sharp sometimes, I'm afraid."

She pulled the cap off her fountain pen and handed Blackwell a copy of the first contract. She met his gaze and found him studying her.

"Your son's comment about a real town," he said. "I take that to mean you're not from around here?"

Candace slid her briefcase aside. "I am, yes, originally. Charles, quite obviously, is not." She rolled her eyes and shook her head, wondering again if this move had been right. Thus far nothing about it had really been the way she'd envisioned. "We just moved back here a couple of months ago. From LA. My son seems to be suffering city withdrawal."

Blackwell nodded and lifted his steaming mug of coffee to his lips. "What brought you back here, if you don't mind my asking?"

Actually, she did mind a little. How did you tell people you came back home to try to correct a whole pile of mistakes?

She shrugged, wanting to say something superficial and get on with the work. But something about the rancher's warm and seemingly genuine interest made her tell more.

"I thought it would be good for my son," she said. "And... for me. I'd been concentrating on building a name for myself ever since I got out of law school. Now I'm going to concentrate on building a life. When I made the decision to get out of the rat race, moving back to Cedar Grove seemed like it might be a good place to start."

"Ah," the rancher said, nodding with something that looked like understanding laced with approval.

Candace chewed the inside of her cheek, wondering if Clint Blackwell had been through something similar himself. Because when she'd tried to explain the whole complicated thing to Eric, she'd seen no glint of comprehension there.

"God, Candace," he'd said, "get a grip. You're regressing, that's all. Things haven't been easy here, so you're wanting to run home and lick your wounds. Listen, sweetheart . . ."

And then he'd tried to come over and hug her, in a very civilized, nineties'-divorce sort of way.

But Candace had begun to realize she might not be such a nineties sort of gal.

"Don't call me 'sweetheart,'" she'd said, and that was pretty much that. She hadn't seen him since. She'd stayed in the bedroom when Eric had come over to tell Charles goodbye. Civility was fine, but it never lasted more than five minutes between them, anyway. Amazing how two people who had once been so alike were now so different. They'd become something of a human oxymoron. Eric, Candace thought, represented the "moron" part nicely.

"So," Clint Blackwell said, setting down his coffee, "how's the big move working out?"

"All right," Candace said, but knew it was time to get down to business. Odd that this meeting had taken such a personal turn. Then again, maybe not, considering Charles's opening gambits. "We're still adjusting to the change, but I'm optimistic that it'll all work out. Now, Mr. Blackwell, on page three of this first set of papers, Jack has marked the fourth paragraph as something he wanted us to go over."

"Okay," Blackwell said, straightening in his chair, taking his cue.

Candace could see more questions in his eyes, more interest in her situation—and maybe even in her.

She glanced at his hands, but saw no wedding band.

The contracts required his signature only.

He also didn't *seem* like a married man, and she found herself regretting that.

Because she liked Clint Blackwell.

But the little undercurrents of chemistry she was beginning to feel running between them would be reason enough that they could never become friends.

"Okay, Charles," Candace said, after dinner that night, "this is the deal. I've been letting you get away with murder since we moved here because I know you're not very happy about it."

"I hate it here," Charles said, blinking at her through his glasses.

"I know you do," Candace said. "Now. But if you just give it a chance—"

Charles, on the sofa, crossed his arms, shutting her out.

Candace stopped pacing the living room, rubbed her hands over her face and sighed.

"If you keep it up," she said quietly, "you're going to get expelled. Charles, that's a pretty big deal. Is that what you want?"

"I want to go back to my old school," Charles said. "I want to go back to California."

So do I, Candace thought. *Right this minute, so do I.*

She'd never dreamed the move would be this hard. Or that Cedar Grove, "home," was really no longer home at all. With her parents gone, killed nearly three years ago, and no other family to speak of, the town had metamorphosed in her absence.

Now the town was just a town. And home was . . . well, a place sixteen years in the past, a Norman Rockwell painting in the mind. It made her feel stunningly bereft and rootless. And more alone than she'd ever felt in her life. If *she* felt that way, how much worse it must be for Charles.

"Give it six months," Candace said, and Charles stared at her.

"What?"

Candace took a deep breath. This was the first time she'd admitted aloud, to herself or to Charles, that this might not be the place they would stay. That this might have been a mistake. That they might both be better off back in LA.

"Six months," Candace said. "If you'll straighten up and quit getting in trouble at school and honestly try to make an effort to make friends and like Cedar

Grove, I'll ask you in six months, and if you still hate it, we'll talk about moving back.''

"You mean it?" Charles asked.

Candace nodded. "But only if you really try, Charles. You're not going to get me to do anything by fighting me every inch of the way.''

"All right," Charles said. "Six months." He pushed himself off the couch and walked over to Candace and held out his small hand.

She took it, shook it and wondered if this, too, had been a mistake.

Still, it was the first thing she'd tried that seemed to really reach her son in a long time. And if he would really quit fighting the change, she was sure he'd begin to discover for himself all the charms their new life could hold.

"It's a deal, then?" she said.

Charles nodded. "Deal."

When he went off to play with his computer before bed, Candace had the feeling that the breakthrough she'd been looking for had finally come.

At what cost, she wasn't sure. But anything had to be better than the last few months.

Dear Dad,

We'll be moving back home next fall, by October or so. Mom says if I still hate it here by then, we can move back. Don't tell her I told you, because she thinks I'll change my mind, but I won't. But I *will* stick to my part of the bargain and stay out of trouble until then. I want to come home. This place is a hick, nowhere little town, just like you said. I think Mom's starting to see that, too.

Say hello to Gina and everybody for me.

See you soon.

Your son,
Charles

Chapter Three

He couldn't stop thinking about them—Candace Whitney and her son. Something about the two of them intrigued him as nothing had in a while. Maybe it was the kid, little "Charles," and his quick and cynical mind. Or maybe it was the mother; beautiful, confident, polished and professional...yet feeling the weight of big problems right now.

He'd seen it in her eyes, flashes of weariness, flashes of fear. She wanted to make a better life for her son but had to be wondering if the trauma of the move was for better or worse.

She had guts and strength, and Clint admired that. He was also a sucker for a damsel in distress and kept thinking there had to be something he could do to help lighten the load.

"Collins, Harden and Smith," the receptionist said, on the other end of the phone.

"Hi, Melissa. This is Clint Blackwell. Is Jack in?"

While the receptionist buzzed Jack's office, Clint drummed his fingers on the kitchen countertop, wondering how he was going to work the subject around to what he wanted to know.

He started on the pretext of something he'd forgotten to ask the other day. Then he said, "By the way, I was impressed by your Ms. Whitney, Jack. I didn't know you guys had added anyone to the firm."

And Jack being Jack, that was all it took.

"Candace? Oh, yeah, she's great. A little quiet and overly somber for my taste, but a darned good lawyer. Too good, for what we've got her doing, I'll tell you that. She was with some hotshot firm out in LA, but said she didn't want that kind of work anymore. Said she moved here after her divorce to get away from all that. Wanted to spend her time and energy on her kid. And that kid! Jeez! You wouldn't believe the stuff that kid puts her through. The principal, Pete Drake over at Elm Street, calls here half a dozen times a week...."

Ah, Clint thought, nodding his head. *Bingo.*

The next call he made was to Peter Drake, principal of little Charles's school, and Clint's longtime sports rival and friend. There were advantages to living in a small town; knowing half the population was sometimes one of them.

"Blackwell," Peter Drake said, a grin in his voice. "I didn't expect to hear from you until spring games started. What's on your little mind?"

"Plenty, as usual," Clint said. "I wanted to tell you I've got some new guys for the church team this year. Real talent, Pete. As a friend, I thought it was only fair to warn you that Cedar Grove Congregational is going to beat the pants off First Methodist."

"*You* say," Drake taunted. Then, curious, he asked, "Who've you got?"

Clint laughed and told him about Bobby, Ray, Ian and Dean, three of whom Pete Drake had had in his school a few years back.

"Those delinquents?" Drake said. "I don't remember any of them being athletic. They were too worried about sneaking a smoke and cutting class to have time for much else—and that was in fifth grade! Now—"

"Now," Clint said, "they're changing every day. Now they want to be on the ball team. First, though, they've got to get used to the idea of going to church. You know what Randall says. No pray, no play."

"Such discrimination," Drake drawled. "And from a man of the cloth."

"World's going to hell in a hand basket," Clint said. "By the way, Pete, there was something I wanted to get your take on. A kid I met the other day that goes to your school. He struck me as kind of...unusual for a first-grader. His name's—"

"A first-grader?" Drake said. "Unusual? That would be—"

"Charles—" Clint said.

"Whitney," Drake finished.

Clint laughed. "What can you tell me about him?"

In the next five minutes, Peter Drake told him plenty.

"Why all the interest, Clint? You thinking about adding a six-year-old to your Brat Pack?"

"Not really," Clint said. "He just left me intrigued—nosy, I guess. I just wanted to find out the whole story."

"He could be a great kid," Drake said. "But he's hiding most of the good stuff behind a lot of anger, confusion and pain. How'd you meet him?"

"His mother handled some legal work for me. The day of our appointment, she had to bring Charles along. I got the impression that the boy hasn't adjusted to the move."

"He won't *let* himself adjust," Drake said. "I think he feels that if he does, he'll lose his father completely, but if he hangs on to the past and refuses to go on, he'll keep his father somehow."

"They must have been close," Clint said, feeling for both the boy and the father. If Clint had a son, he couldn't imagine being separated by half a country.

"I don't think so," Drake said. "Judging by Charles himself, and by what I've gleaned from the mother, I think it was just the opposite of what you'd expect. Apparently the Whitneys were separated six months before Candace actually made the move—and pretty much estranged even before that.

"That's what threw Candace so much when they first got here. Charles and his father had barely seen each other for the last year, and the boy hadn't seemed to be bothered that much. Then, after the move, all the kid can talk about is his dad and going home. Candace told me one day that if her ex-husband and son really had been close, she wouldn't have considered taking Charles away in the first place, but that the way things were, with Mr. Whitney so busy with his career and new girlfriend, he barely had time for Charles at all. She thought it'd be good to get him away from the rejection."

"Nice guy," Clint said.

"Cream of the ever-lovin' crop," Drake said. "And there's a million more out there just like him. You want to know where your problem kids come from?"

"It's a crummy world out there," Clint said.

"And the ones who suffer most are our children." After a long second Drake said, "Do me a favor, Clint. Try your hand with Charles. You've done some fine work with your other hoodlums. I think you might have a chance at getting through to him, too."

"I don't know anything about six-year-olds," Clint said. And the Whitneys' problems ran deeper than he'd really expected. The more he heard, the more his instincts screamed at him to leave it alone, leave *them* alone, because he'd be getting in way over his head. He wasn't a trained therapist; he was a simple rancher who had worked with a handful of troubled kids and succeeded thus far by virtue of trial and error. Hardly a record with which to go tromping into the Whitney mine field.

"Don't think of Charles as a six-year-old," Peter Drake said. "Think of him as a pint-size delinquent, because if something doesn't happen for him, I feel very sure that that's what he'll be. I told Frieda the other day that I dearly hoped Charles Whitney doesn't take up smoking. I'll go see him on visiting days, but I *won't* bring him cigarettes."

"Not funny," Clint said, his mouth quirking wryly.

"I know," Drake said. "Morgue humor. Keeps doctors, morticians and grade school principals sane. What do you say, Blackwell? Can't hurt to try. Shall I give Mother of Frankenstein a call and set things up?"

"What makes you think she'll be receptive to the idea?"

"I told her last week I was at the point where I might have to expel her son."

Clint whistled through his teeth, letting this sink in. "All right," he said. "If she's up for giving it a try, I guess I am. If nothing else, maybe I can show Charles how to lighten up and have a little fun."

"That would be a good step," Drake said. "Right now he acts like a stodgy little accountant. I'll call Candace as soon as I hang up."

"If she's receptive, tell her to give me a call and we can talk about it more."

"Will do," Drake said. "And thanks. Both Frieda and I lie awake nights trying to think of ways to get through to that kid."

"Yeah? And how do you know what Frieda Dale is doing with her nights—or would that be telling?" Clint asked, wondering if the shy principal had finally won his ladylove.

"That," Drake said, "would be none of your business."

Clint laughed, and Peter Drake hung up. Clint stood by the kitchen phone for a minute, remembering his words. *I lie awake nights trying to think of ways to get through to that kid.*

Clint had the feeling that now he'd be doing the same thing.

The front door rattled and Candace set the briefs she'd been working on aside. She took off her reading glasses and rose to greet Charles as he came in.

The April breeze had nipped his cheeks and tousled his straight blond hair. Love washed over her, and she felt indecision flare. Peter Drake had persuaded her to try his idea, but now she wondered if she might be doing the wrong thing—or the okay thing for all the wrong reasons. She didn't want to get weak here all of a sudden and do something just because it would be so wonderful to let someone else help shoulder the load. She also didn't want to *not* do something that might help her son.

"Hi, sweetie," she said, going over to take his coat. "How was school today?"

Charles shrugged, dropping his books on the couch. "Okay. Still boring, but okay."

That was at least an improvement over the past two months. Prior to their bargain of last week, Charles's answers had been long and full of derision and complaints. The teachers were dense, the other kids were babies, and even the fifth-graders didn't know how to use a computer. Following this sort of thing, *boring but okay* was a glowing compliment.

"No trouble?" Candace said.

"No." Charles pushed his glasses up on his nose and studied Candace, knowing something new was up. He was so perceptive, so sensitive to changing moods and underlying meanings. This was a child who, at four, had tried to soothe Candace because he'd understood some of the implications of his daddy having a girl-friend, a fact they'd thought they'd kept inaccessible from their small son.

"I talked to Mr. Drake today," she said, brushing absently at the sleeve of his tweed coat.

"I didn't do anything," Charles said, bristling.

"I know. He said your attitude seemed much better this week. He and Mrs. Dale are very pleased."

"He and Mrs. Dale have the hots for each other."

"Charles!"

Charles shifted, lowered his gaze. "Well, they do. That's what all the kids say."

"The first-graders say that?"

He shrugged. "I don't know. It might be the bigger kids. Anyway, it's true. Whenever Mr. Drake comes in the room, Mrs. Dale just stares at him. Do you figure that means Mrs. Dale is going to get a divorce, too?"

Candace felt her temples throb. Guilt and remorse and regret swamped her anew. "Mrs. Dale is a widow, Charles. That means her husband died. Listen, about my conversation with Mr. Drake. We got to talking, and it turns out he knows Mr. Blackwell."

Charles's mouth quirked. "Clinty?"

Candace grimaced. "That's 'Mister' to you, buster."

"He said he liked it."

"He was playing with you, Charles."

"Anyway," Charles said, "what about him?" Curious, he watched her as he plopped onto the couch, short legs still very far from touching the floor.

"Well," Candace said, suddenly nervous about the subterfuge, "Mr. Drake and I are so pleased with the way you're giving Cedar Grove a chance, we started talking about giving you some sort of a . . . reward."

"Yeah?" Charles perked up. "How much?"

Candace sighed. "It's not money, Charles. It's fun—and a new experience. Mr. Drake set it up with Mr. Blackwell for you to go out to the Double C and learn how to ride a horse!"

"Oh," Charles said, and raised his eyebrows in that way that said she surely must be addled. "Riding a horse. That's the reward?"

"Yes," Candace said evenly. "I thought it would be nice if you got out and did something new and fun."

"Oh," Charles said again, watching her too closely—trying to determine if this horse-riding thing was an option or an order. "That's okay, Mom," he said, hopping down off the couch and giving her a grin, "I don't need a reward. I'm just doing my part of our deal." *And in six months, you can do your part, too. Because I might go along and humor you on this, but I'm* never *going to like it here.* Charles left that unspoken, but Candace heard the sentiment clearly.

She suddenly wanted to cry.

What was the matter with this child? Between herself and Eric, what had they done?

Didn't every little kid want to ride a horse? Dream of being a cowboy and riding the range?

And didn't every little kid like snowball fights and wading in creeks and skipping flatties across farm ponds?

All these things and more Candace had tried to get Charles to go out and do with her since they'd moved back, these things she remembered so cleanly and clearly from her own childhood with all its simple and innocent magic: jumping in mountains of crackly fall leaves; making rope swings in hay lofts.

But not one of these things had appealed to her son. Candace had finally gotten the message when Charles asked if she wanted to change his name to Opie and hers to Aunt Bea.

What had they done?

And what else, Candace wondered, had they stolen from their son that he might never get back?

"Listen to me, Charles," Candace said, and found herself trembling. "You're going out to the Double C. You're going out to that ranch on Saturday morning, and like it or not, Charles, you're *going to have fun!* Do you understand me?"

Charles ran his tongue along his back teeth, wanting to argue this ridiculous point. Then he thought better of it, lifted his chin, met her gaze.

"All right," he said. "Now may I be excused? I'd like to go to my room."

"Yes," Candace said and suddenly felt exhausted, as if all the hard months had come at this moment to settle on her at once. "Yes, Charles, you may."

When he'd gone, she sank into the corner of the cream leather couch and put her head in her hands.

She'd thought gaining Charles's compliance would make everything right. Instead she felt even more like the villain and now had a suffering martyr for a son.

He would grit his teeth and do whatever would make her happy.

But this wasn't about making her *happy,* was it?

It was all *supposed* to be about making a better, cleaner, more decent and meaningful life for her son.

Dear Crystal,

My mother is making me do something this Saturday that made me think of you. Sort of.

She's making me go out to this hick ranch and learn how to ride a horse. They'll probably make me wear a goofy hat and say Yeehah! too.

But it made me think of something. Doesn't your uncle have the polo ponies? If I learn to ride here, maybe I can learn to play polo with you this year when I move back.

See you soon, and say hi to everybody at school.

Your friend stuck in the sticks,
Charles

On Friday night Clint Blackwell called to confirm their plans for the next morning.

Candace had spent the week vacillating between sticking to the plan and canceling. After all, Charles was complying with her wishes and had had no more trouble at school. He was whizzing through his work and impressing Mrs. Dale. He was following the rules and earning extra privileges because of it.

Now that he was trying to work with the system rather than fight it, Mrs. Dale and Peter Drake were doing things to work with him. For one, they'd agreed to make special arrangements for him to get some computer lab time—a course of study heretofore reserved for the sixth-graders. They had also changed Charles's English text from *Run Spot Run!* to *The Hardy Boys* and some of Dickens. Charles had said he'd heard *The Count of Monte Cristo* was good, and

Frieda Dale had called to see if Candace wanted to give that a try.

Charles seemed a bit happier about all of this and his situation in general. Still, though, he went about his part of the bargain with the grim determination of a prisoner bucking for parole.

He was doing things but not liking them.

And according to Peter Drake and Clint Blackwell, the first goal out at the Double C would be to help Charles learn how to have fun.

"Can you do that?" Candace had said, remembering her own attempts.

"All we can do is try," both Clint and Drake had responded.

"But if we can crack through Charles's pseudo-adult cynicism and sophistication, I would think it would change that little boy's life."

And this statement, made by Drake, was the one that kept coming back to mind.

So when Clint Blackwell called on Friday, Candace said, "Yes. I guess we'll be there."

"You *guess?*" Blackwell said. "Having second thoughts?"

"Second and third and fourth," Candace said. "It just feels so strange ordering my son to do something for fun."

Blackwell chuckled, and at the warm sound of it, Candace felt herself smiling, as well.

"I guess it's tough to be a parent," Clint said. "But as long as he still does what you tell him, you've got the chance to make a change. It's these teenagers who realize they don't *have* to do anything who make things really tough.''

"Well, I don't have that situation yet," Candace said. "Actually, he's doing every single thing I say."

"Sticking to his part of the bargain," Clint said.

"Yes. So I won't have any grounds not to leave in six months. Today he allowed me to buy him some new boots and jeans. Tomorrow he'll allow you to set him up on a horse. To tell you the truth, Mr. Blackwell, this stoic-submissive stuff is getting on my nerves. I almost wish I could have my old argumentative son back."

Clint laughed again. "I wouldn't worry about that, Mrs. Whitney. I'm sure you'll see that side of young Charles again before long."

"Call me Candace," she said, feeling suddenly and oddly close to this man who wanted to help her son. "Please."

"And I'm Clint," he said. "For both you and Charles. The less formality between me and the kids, the more progress I seem to make."

"Okay," Candace said. "Well, I guess we'll see you tomorrow about nine."

"Good," Clint said. "And by the way. After the first few minutes, I think it'd be best if you make some excuse and then go ahead and leave—"

"Leave?" Candace said, startled by the idea.

"Or go up to the house if you want," Blackwell said. "Or sit in the car."

"But—"

"Look, Candance," Clint said. "It's nothing against you, but Charles and I have to have a chance to come to an understanding of our own, form our own relationship without input from anybody else. Do you see what I'm saying?"

"I—"

"In other words," Clint said, "I want Charles to be able to speak freely without getting in trouble. If his mother is standing there, that's not going to happen. The sooner we get down to him dealing with me honestly, the sooner the progress comes. Make sense?"

Actually, it did, Candace had to admit. Though she hadn't thought about it before, of course her immediate presence would be counterproductive.

"Makes sense," she said. "Well, I guess I'll bring a book or something. I'll leave you two alone, but I don't think I'm quite ready to go off and leave him at the ranch."

Especially when he didn't want to go there in the first place. And with her not around . . . Charles undoubtedly wasn't interested in pleasing Clint Blackwell. His "deal" was with Candace. No, for a variety of reasons, she didn't think it wise to get too far away.

Plus, horses were big, powerful animals. And if Charles got scared or something, she wanted to be there to put an end to the experiment. There was a difference between tough love and traumatizing a child. While she felt good about Clint Blackwell, and

Peter Drake had recommended him highly, how could she know if he'd know where to draw the line?

"You just don't trust me," Blackwell said, and Candace blinked, startled that he'd essentially read her mind.

"No, it's not that. Not exactly. It's just—"

"I know what it is," Blackwell said. "You think I'm going to dunk your six-year-old in the watering trough like I did Ian the other day. I'm crushed, Candace, that you could think that of me."

Then she realized, of course, that he was teasing her. *And* trying to let her know he didn't blame her for wondering and that he understood her concerns, but that they weren't warranted. He was dealing with a small child and knew it. There was, in his mind, a huge difference between little Charles and the boys she'd seen him horsing around with the other day.

"Actually, I hadn't thought about the watering trough," Candace said, smiling. "Thank you for giving me something else to worry about."

But the truth was she was beginning to feel very good about this whole situation. Clint Blackwell liked and was interested in helping her son make this huge adjustment. He had a track record with kids and the principal at Charles's school thought he was wonderful. He seemed kind and warm and long on integrity. And he also seemed to Candace to be very, very strong.

So did that mean she was weak for wanting to lean on him like this?

Maybe not. Maybe it just meant she was lucky and had finally found the right person for this very important job.

"I'll see you tomorrow," Clint Blackwell said warmly.

Candace was still smiling when she gently hung up the phone.

"Mom?" Charles stood in her bedroom doorway, sleep-rumpled and huge eyed without his glasses.

"Did I wake you up, honey?" Candace said. "I'm sorry."

"Who was on the phone?" Charles asked, climbing up beside her on the bed.

"Mr. Blackwell. He called to make sure we were still coming tomorrow morning."

Charles's face fell. "Oh," he said softly. "I heard it ring. I thought it might be Dad."

Chapter Four

It was a mistake; she knew it the minute she saw him. He was tall and tanned and lean, and the small tinglings of attraction she'd felt the other day hit her this day like live electric current.

Last week she'd been stressed and tired and preoccupied. This week she was fresh and rested and nervously optimistic.

Today, he struck her as, quite possibly, the most attractive man she'd ever seen. Now that they were sharers in this problem of her son, now that they were no longer attorney and client, Candace was startled to feel impulses awaken which had been forced into long slumber.

"Good morning," he said, and the sound of his voice, whiskey-rough, rubbed over her newly sensitized nerve endings like good velvet.

"Hello," she managed, and wondered why her senses were so suddenly running amok. This wasn't like her, wasn't like her at all.

And the last thing she was interested in right now was a relationship with a man. Charles had suffered enough pain and rejection with his own father. Candace had made up her mind long ago that she would never complicate things the way Eric had by bringing in a new love interest. If she and Eric couldn't make things work, that was one thing. But, chemistry and loneliness and things physical aside, she would *not* make things harder for her son by adding a boyfriend to the whole jumbled-up mess.

"Hey, Charles," Clint Blackwell said, flashing a white grin, "I see you're all outfitted. Jeans. Boots. You almost look like a regular cowboy. Now all you need is a hat."

At this, Clint Blackwell removed his own felt Stetson and dropped it onto Charles's head.

It dropped below the boy's eye level, but Candace caught the wince of distaste, the finicky curl of his small upper lip.

Before Charles could say something insulting, she gripped his upper arm in warning.

Clint, watching mother and son, ran his tongue along the inside of his cheek.

This was just what he'd been talking about—parental interference. While he knew it was Candace's job to guide her son, he now had a job to do, too. And he didn't want Charles's tempered reactions; he wanted his real ones. Throw things at a kid and watch him react—you soon had a strong sense of what made him tick.

Slowly Charles poked the brim of the hat up with one index finger. Clint retrieved the Stetson and put it back on his own head.

"Sorry, partner," he said, winking. "Bad fit." Then he turned to Candace. "Okay, Mom," Clint said, "I think Charles and I can handle things from here."

Candace looked at him, surprised that he wanted her to take off so soon.

Don't fight me on this, Clint urged silently. I have a gut feeling about me and this kid. A feeling that had been growing ever since he'd first talked to Candace on the phone.

Given time and opportunity, he knew he could really connect with this child. Knew in that way that you knew when you could feel it down deep in your bones.

Looking at Candace, he had a jolt of sensation, too. But that was different, something better left unexplored. Charles wasn't the only one wounded in the family split.

But, Clint reminded himself, Charles is the only one you're in any position to help. Because the last thing any woman fresh out of a divorce needed was a new man. There was vulnerability there, and a need for space and time. Besides, Clint could tell right now that if he ever got involved with Candace Whitney, things would go much deeper than he wanted them to go.

He remembered thinking of the Whitneys as a mine field, and of getting in way over his head.

That didn't have to happen, but he needed to remember how easily it could. Forewarned is forearmed. And as long as he kept potential pitfalls in mind, he could avoid them. His purpose in all this, his *only* purpose, was to try to connect with an unhappy kid.

He did that every day with the boys, and he could do that here. And the sooner he got the child alone, the sooner he could begin.

He looked at Candace, who was glancing around, uncertain where to go or what to do.

"If you want, you can go up to the house," Clint said. "Alice, my housekeeper, is baking pies."

"I wouldn't want to get in the way," Candace said. "I brought a book. I could just sit in the car... or something."

"Whatever suits you," Clint said. "But I told Alice you might be in. She said she'd like the company. You've got to watch her, though. She's got thirty pies to bake for the church bake sale tomorrow. If you get anywhere close, she'll probably put you to work. Which is why I planned to spend my day outside. My darned pie crust is just never quite flaky."

Candace grinned, suddenly more at ease. "Well," she said, "in that case, maybe I will go in. Sounds like your Alice could use a little help."

"You can't make pies, either, Mom," Charles said. "The time you tried to make that pecan pie, it exploded all over the oven."

Candace grimaced. "Yes, and thank you for telling everyone about that, Charles." She shrugged and gave a lopsided smile that Clint found endearing in a hotshot lady lawyer. "I can measure and stir and clean up," she said. "I'll leave the actual pie baking to the seasoned professional."

She was still smiling when she turned to go, and Clint's gaze lingered for a few seconds, watching after her. The morning sun caught in her auburn hair and turned it bronze. Clint felt his senses stir and turned to Charles to put a stop to that trend.

"So?" Charles Whitney said when his mother was mounting the porch steps—and safely out of earshot. "Where's the horse? I'm only doing this because my mother's making me, so I'd like to get it over with."

The boy crossed his arms and stood tapping his booted foot.

Clint rubbed a hand over his mouth to hide a wry grin.

With his mother gone, there would be no coaxing required to get Charles Whitney to speak his mind.

Hey ho, Clint thought, with the same sense of anticipation he had when climbing onto a green horse to break it. Ready or not, here we go. . . .

"It smells heavenly in here," Candace said while Alice poured her a cup of coffee in the big, warm kitchen. It was all honey pine and golden oak, with a hardwood floor scattered with hand-tied rag rugs, and pie tins and makings taking up the counters. "Clint said you were baking thirty pies?"

"Thirty-one," Alice said. "Thanks to Clint."

She set the coffee in front of Candace at the table, then went back to sifting flour into a mixing bowl. She was a trim woman, sixtyish, who wore faded denims, a red flannel shirt and a white baker's apron. On her feet were scuffed tan cowboy boots, age indeterminate. She looked more like a ranch hand than a housekeeper and, bemused by this, Candace liked her on sight.

"What kind are you making?" Candace asked, wrapping both hands around the warm mug.

"Eight cherry, six pumpkin, twelve apple, four raisin, and one blueberry. Clint slipped that last request in when he found out I was baking today. Blueberry's his favorite. Can't stand it myself."

But she was obviously very fond of her employer, Candace thought. She smiled and drank some of the coffee. It was hot and strong and made her think of cowboys out on the trail.

"As soon as I finish this, I'm ready and willing to help," Candace said. "I have to admit I haven't done much baking in quite a while, but I'm a quick study and usually do all right under close supervision."

"That's good enough for me," Alice said and thunked a wooden spoon against the glass bowl to make a clump of shortening drop off. She glanced up out the kitchen window and paused in her work.

"Hey," Alice said, grinning, "come look at this. This is a big moment in your son's life. The little boy from the big city is meeting his first horse. It's a regular Kodak moment, Candace. Come see for yourself."

"His name's Coyote," Clint said, holding the horse's head by the halter strap.

Charles snorted. "He's a horse. Why would you name him Coyote?"

"Well, when he was first born, he took one look at that big old full moon and got fascinated. For weeks after, he'd stretch his scrawny neck toward the moon and whinny at it every night. Just like a—"

"Coyote," Charles said. "I think you're making that up."

But he did actually seem intrigued by the tale, and Clint felt encouraged by that. Thus far it was the first thing about this day in which Charles seemed to take any interest at all.

"Where's the saddle?" Charles said, frowning. "How can you ride a horse without a saddle?"

"You can ride a horse bareback, hotshot," Clint said. "But you're not going to. And you don't just jump on a horse and ride him, anyway. A horse is a living thing, and he has feelings, too. He's not like a motorcycle or a bike. You have to get to know him, talk to him a little, treat him with respect. You see, most people don't realize that riding a horse is a two-way proposition. You understand what I'm saying, Charles?"

"Yes," Charles said, shifting his weight to the other foot. "You're saying this whole horse-riding thing could take all day."

"That's it," Alice said, nodding near Candace's shoulder. "Just cut the shortening into the flour. Don't mush it up. Learning how to cut it just right is what makes it flaky."

From where she stood, Candace could work on the pie crust and keep one eye on Charles at the same time. She watched as Clint Blackwell showed him how to stroke the horse's nose, and Candace recalled that a horse's nose felt just like warm velvet.

She remembered going riding in her own childhood: the warmth of the powerful horse; muscles bunching and stretching; the horsey smell that clung to your clothes and skin even after a hot bath. The pleasantly sore muscles that lingered for days and reminded you of the ride. The picnics they'd carried in squeaky leather saddlebags. The way they'd pretended they were the early pioneers and no one had ever blazed that trail before.

The memory was exciting and evocative to Candace. She knew it would be a great way for a kid to spend a day. Once Charles got started, even he couldn't hold out against the romance of it all.

"He's going to love it," Candace murmured to Alice, sure once again that coming out here today had not been a mistake after all. "There's nothing like a horse when you're a kid."

"This looks like a lot of work to me," Charles said, as Clint hefted the saddle onto Coyote and showed Charles how to tighten the cinch strap.

"Work?" Clint said. "Saddling a horse isn't work. It's a pleasure."

"Why?"

Clint thought about that. By this point he'd really expected Charles to begin to get involved. He'd also thought the boy's disinterest was probably feigned, an outward show of boredom that hid an inner excitement. Now, though, he wasn't so sure. This little six-year-old didn't seem to be faking.

"It's a pleasure," Clint said, "because a good horse is a cowboy's best friend. He's someone to talk to, someone to keep you company—someone who could save your life. When you have a best friend, you enjoy taking good care of him. Like a dog. You ever have a dog, Charles?"

"No."

Clint checked the saddle blanket again, smoothing a wrinkle. "How about a cat?"

"No."

He pulled the leather strap tight and looped it through the ring. "A hamster?"

"No. We have a gerbil at school, but I think keeping it in that little cage is cruel."

"You might have a point there," Clint said, tying off the strap. He lowered the stirrup and turned to look at Charles. "You've never had any kind of a pet?"

"I had some fish for a while," Charles said.

Clint shook his head. "No, I mean like a *real* pet, something you had to really take care of."

Charles shrugged. "I took care of my fish, but I took too good a care of them. I fed them too much, and they died."

Clint winced, then reached out to ruffle the boy's blond hair. "Sorry to hear that, sport."

Charles tipped his head back to look up at him. "I think I know what you're talking about, though, taking care of your best friend. I enjoy taking care of my computer."

Clint looked at the boy, then sighed. "Your computer," he said. "Right. Come on, Charles. I think you're ready to ride."

"He's getting on," Candace said, leaning forward over the sink. "Oh, look, Alice, he's getting on."

Suddenly the big bay horse looked huge—and Charles tiny. "Why isn't Clint getting on with him?" Candace said. "Charles can't ride that horse alone!"

She dropped her lump of pie dough back into the bowl and reached for a towel to wipe her hands.

"Wait," Alice said, putting a restraining hand on her arm. "Clint knows what he's doing. He won't take any chances with your boy."

"But Charles is only—"

"Just trust him," Alice said.

Easy to say, but not at all easy to do.

Still, Candace tried. The pies were forgotten as she gripped the edges of the counter and watched Clint Blackwell instruct her son.

"How are the stirrups?" Clint asked, standing next to Charles as he sat on the horse.

"O-okay, I guess," Charles said, trying to be blasé, but stammering a little.

He was nervous, and Clint was actually glad to see this. Any break in the boy's indifference was a very good sign.

"Now don't be scared," Clint said. "Coyote is a good horse, and I'm not going to turn you loose until you're ready."

"I'm not ready," Charles said, wide-eyed. His knuckles were white as he gripped the saddle horn with both hands. "Clint—please—don't let him go."

Ah, Clint thought, putting a hand on the boy's back to reassure him he was safe. Phase one accomplished. With those two little words, they had broken through the first wall.

Clint—please...

Charles needed him right now—and knew it. And, most important, he was in a situation where he didn't mind showing it. Clint's mouth quirked wryly. Nothing like a little good, old-fashioned terror to bring two people together.

"I won't let him go," Clint said, keeping one hand on Charles and the other on Coyote's reins. He had intended to lead the horse around the corral, figuring the last thing Charles would want was to have his personal space invaded by Clint riding with him. Now, however, things might have changed.

"I usually ride with people the first time," he said casually. "Do you want to do it that way, or would you rather I lead him around for you?"

"I...I think I'd *rather* get off," Charles said, still hanging on for dear life to the horse who was standing calmly.

Clint tried to keep his expression neutral, but he hated the turn things had just taken. He would never make a scared kid stay on a horse. Still, if Charles got off now, Clint knew he'd never get on one again.

"Well," he said, "if that's the way you really feel about it..." He moved to the left and lifted his arms to help the child down.

"I do," Charles said, nodding vehemently. "But...I promised my mom." He licked his lips, looked down at Clint from his height in the saddle. "I have to ride today," he said. "If you usually ride with people the first time, then maybe that's the way we should do it."

Clint grinned, liking the way the boy had conquered his fear. *And* the fact that he did want to try this horse-riding thing after all. Because Clint knew as well as Charles that if the boy climbed down right now, his mother wouldn't be angry or disappointed—she'd be supportive and tell him he gave it a good try.

"Good for you, Charlie," Clint said, grinning up at him. "I'm beginning to think you're not such a weenie after all."

Charles blinked, so shocked by this he forgot to take offense at not being called Charles.

Then, just before Clint swung himself up to sit behind the saddle, he saw the pleased expression that came to the boy's face.

Hey, I'm not a weenie! that look said. I've conquered my fears and now I'm going to ride this big old horse.

Clint, now sitting behind Charles, wore the same sort of bemused and pleased look, too. He realized they'd come a heckuva long way this morning without even leaving the corral.

As he reached around Charles and gathered the reins, he knew they were both riding high and tall. Nothing like the pride of accomplishment to get things underway.

He could hardly wait to tell Candace—or to see the warm glow of pleasure he knew he'd be responsible for bringing to her face.

"You see?" Alice said. "Nothing to worry about. With Clint up there, nothing can happen to your son."

Candace let out a long breath. She hadn't realized she'd been holding herself so tense. What was the matter with her? Clint Blackwell wasn't an idiot. Of course he knew how to keep a child safe.

She laughed and felt thrilled for Charles as she watched the two walk the big bay around the corral.

They did this for three or four laps, and then Candace saw Clint look toward one of the barns and gesture to someone.

A minute later a dark-haired youth appeared. Ian, Candace thought. The boy Clint had dunked in the watering trough.

Clint, still atop the horse, said something to Ian and gestured to the corral fence.

An instant later, Candace realized he'd actually been gesturing toward the gate.

She felt the muscles tighten again as Ian opened the gate and Blackwell and Charles rode the big horse through.

"Where do you suppose they're going?" Candace murmured to Alice.

"Out riding," Alice said, rolling out pie dough. "Let's get to work," she suggested. "Now that those two have started, they could be gone all day."

Candace groaned, not wanting Charles out of her sight.

Still, as she watched them ride off to the west, the sight of the big man behind the little boy took most of the edge off her anxiety.

Charles would be safe. Clint would see to that.

She thought about his arms reaching around Charles to both guard the child and hold the reins. She thought about those strong arms and couldn't help wondering how she'd feel if she were sitting where Charles was. . . .

But no.

She would *not* entertain ridiculous thoughts like that.

As they rounded a corner and disappeared behind an outbuilding, Candace grabbed a rolling pin and put her energies into flattening a mound of dough.

She'd been thinking about Clint Blackwell a lot this morning, and she realized that the only reason she was interested in him as a man was that he'd become something of a . . . hero to her. There was nothing else to this ridiculous and sudden attraction. Nothing at all.

It was simply a natural phenomenon to develop a crush on someone who helps you handle a bad situation, as Blackwell was doing with her and Charles.

The same thing had happened to her friend Morgan back home when she fell suddenly in love with the sixty-year-old divorce lawyer who had won her both the house and a very nice alimony settlement.

The romantic attraction, of course, faded in due time, and Morgan got her emotions back under control.

Candace would, too, once this hero thing wore off. So for the time being she'd tolerate the crush and even understand it as natural and normal, and stop fighting it so hard. It was a phase and would pass. But she would also do nothing to feed it or encourage it to grow.

With that sorted out, she leaned into the rolling pin and ordered her mind to think about her pies—instead of what it might be like to find herself in her new hero's arms.

Chapter Five

"So," Clint said after they'd stuffed themselves on a lunch of Alice's cold fried chicken and warm blueberry pie, "are you going to swing by the bake sale tomorrow? See the fruits of all your labors?"

"Uh," Candace said brilliantly. She'd been sitting there basking in the glow of the morning, and the thought had never crossed her mind. It had been one of those times where the present was enough, and thoughts of what came next seemed gratuitous.

"You should come," Alice said, bringing more coffee to the table. "It's a fun sale. And we're having a potluck fellowship dinner right after church. Then everybody goes to the bake sale and has dessert. You could meet a lot of people—maybe even run into some old friends."

"Sounds like fun," Candace said, remembering similar affairs from her youth. And it would be nice to start meeting people again, getting involved. Until you did that, no place would ever really seem like home. Home was where your life was, she was beginning to realize. And your life was composed, essentially, of who you chose to have in it, and what you chose as your priorities.

She thought about Clint Blackwell and the way he chose to spend his days—working with the land, his livestock and a passel of troubled kids. She sensed in him a fulfillment she'd certainly never seen in Eric. But she didn't think living in Cedar Grove was what made that difference. It was a question of values, she thought. Priorities. And if Clint Blackwell suddenly found himself in LA, Candace couldn't imagine that he'd live his life any differently. It wasn't the place that determined quality of life. It was the person. And Clint Blackwell was...

She looked over and saw him watching her, then, startled and guilty, she quickly looked away. *Get a grip, Candace,* she thought, knowing the voice in her head sounded just like Eric. But if she didn't get a handle on this Clint Blackwell thing, she'd be thinking herself half in love with the man just like Morgan and her lawyer friend.

She focused on Charles, reminding herself that he was the only reason they were here in the first place.

He sat frowning, picking at his pie crust, still thinking about the bake sale, obviously debating whether the concept, foreign to him, did indeed sound like fun or not.

He'd been fairly silent through most of the meal, but more reflective than sullen or surly, and that delighted Candace. He'd eaten well—a compliment to his host and hostess—and not made one snide comment since he and Clint had come back from their ride.

And while he hadn't gone so far as to rave about the experience, he'd come back with his cheeks flushed and his blue eyes more alive and sparkling than she'd seen them for some time.

She suspected he'd had a glorious morning and the ensuing thoughtful air came from a need to sit and reevaluate the reality of his experience versus his preconceptions. *Hey, this hick stuff is fun!* she hoped he would think. And...*Hey, maybe I'll try some of the other things Mom keeps wanting me to try....*

And, just maybe...*Hey, maybe Cedar Grove isn't so bad after all. Maybe in six months, I'll even want to stay....*

But no. That would be pushing things. Candace would content herself with the fact that her son had had a new experience and a wonderful morning. It was a big step, and for now it was more than good enough.

"Yes," she said, looking across the table at Clint Blackwell and feeling warm and happy and very connected to him—but for the right reason and in the right way, she reminded herself. As long as she kept her perspective, there was nothing wrong with feeling good about the man because of what he was doing for her son. "I think we will come to the sale."

"What about the other stuff?" Charles said, letting Alice help him to a second slice of pie.

"What other stuff is that, sport?" Clint asked, a half smile lingering on his mouth.

"You know. The church and dinner Alice was talking about. The stuff you're going to do before the sale."

"Oh," Clint said, raising an eyebrow at Charles's interest. "Well, sure, if it sounds like fun to you. I think it'd be great if you two could come." He glanced at Candace and she saw the gleam of victory and something else in his gray eyes, something that made her skin feel warm all over.

"How about it, Mom?" Clint Blackwell said.

"Yeah, Mom," Charles said.

"We really do have fun," Alice said.

Before she could consider the wisdom of this thing, Candace laughed and heard herself agreeing.

"I guess it's unanimous," she said, and before they left the Double C, Clint got her address and promised to pick them up in the the morning at nine forty-five.

"Well," Candace said, lingering over goodbyes at the car, "thanks for...everything."

"Thank *you*," Clint said. "Both of you. I had a great time."

She stood there for a long moment, caught in his gray gaze as well as in the notion that he really seemed to mean what he'd said. She couldn't believe how good it felt after all these months to have someone actually enjoy and appreciate time spent with her son.

Beside her, Charles fidgeted, and in an antsy way, kicked at the dirt with the narrow toe of his new cowboy boot.

"And thanks," Charles mumbled, avoiding Clint's look, "for letting me ride Coyote."

Candace bit her lip and felt her eyes mist. She looked at Clint and knew he knew what a breakthrough this whole thing was.

He winked, sharing the moment, then leaned down to Charles. "You're welcome, partner. And I think you and Coyote hit it off just fine. If you can remember to take good care of him and treat him with respect, you can come out here and ride him anytime."

"Really?" Charles said, eyes wide.

"Really," Clint said.

There was a charged moment when Candace, shocked, thought Charles was going to actually hug Clint Blackwell. Then the moment passed, and Charles thrust out his little hand instead, shaking on the whole deal like a man.

One day, Candace thought. *My son has become a new person after one day with this man....*

"I'll see you tomorrow morning," Clint said and pulled open the car door.

"Okay," Charles said, climbing in and then buckling up. "Nine forty-five."

As Candace pulled the BMW out of the drive, she thought it seemed a very long time until then.

*   *   *

Dear Dad,

Today I did something new and kind of exciting. Mom made me go out to this ranch and learn how to ride a horse. I went along, because it was part of our bargain. I thought I'd hate it, but I didn't. The horse (his name's Coyote) was big, and at first I was scared, but I made myself do it anyway. I'm glad I did. The rancher (his name's Clint Blackwell) said I did great. He's a pretty nice guy, I guess, and I really like his horse. Maybe when I move back home, I could get one of my own.

And maybe if you can come visit soon, I can show you Coyote and ride him for you.

I thought you called the other night, but Mom said it was Mr. Blackwell. I guess you're pretty busy and everything, and you'll call when you can.

I hope you *can* come visit, though, and see me ride Coyote. Even though we'll be moving back, fall is kind of a long ways away.

Write back soon (or call)

Your son,
Charles

"Mom, does this look okay?" Charles said, coming into her room on Sunday morning.

He'd put on a blue suit and tie and looked so much like Eric dressed for work that Candace caught her breath.

"It looks fine, honey," she said. "Very nice."

He was showered and scrubbed, moussed and combed. And excited. Candace could see it in his eyes.

She realized then that he'd never been to church, not really, and regretted that. Having grown up going to church herself, she recalled it as a good way of life, both spiritually and socially. Why she hadn't stuck to those values when she got out of college, she still didn't know. Of course, she didn't know why she'd done or not done a lot of things in the past fourteen years.

"Come here, kiddo," she said and got up from her dressing table. She straightened Charles's tie, which didn't need straightening, then pulled him to her and hugged him tight.

They were going to be okay. After all the fears and pain and doubts, she was really starting to feel down deep that the two of them were going to be okay.

"Mom!" Charles said, squirming out of her snug grasp.

She'd crinkled his clothes and mussed his hair.

He shook his head, exasperated, and marched back to his room to remousse and comb.

Candace laughed and kept on laughing, and from the other room she heard her son join her.

At nine-forty Clint pulled his pickup up to the curb in front of the Whitney house on Cherry Lane. He'd come into town with his truck full of Alice and her pies, but had dropped them all off first at the church to make room for Candace and Charles. Why he hadn't just suggested they meet him there was a question Clint had been wrestling with all morning.

He turned off the engine and wiped sweaty palms on his slacks. He felt nervous and excited and awkward as a teenager on a first date.

But that was the thing. This *wasn't* a date. Not in any way, shape or form was this a date.

This wasn't even a social occasion, really. Candace Whitney was coming because he'd made progress with her son, and this kind of involvement would be good for the boy.

That's what this was about, Charles. Business, essentially. He'd committed to do some work with the boy; and Candace, of course, was committed to doing anything she could, as well.

He got out of the truck and closed the door. He cleared his throat, took a deep breath and adjusted his attitude. If he kept his perspective and remembered what all this was about, it wouldn't be awkward at all.

He raised his hand to rap on the door, but before knuckles touched wood, the door was swinging open and Candace stood smiling in front of him, slim and stunning in a silky dress of kelly green that made her green eyes even more vivid and her bronzy hair glow.

Clint felt the power of chemistry hit with a force that surprised him.

"Good morning," he said, and heard a huskiness in his voice that he hoped she mistook for the beginnings of a head cold.

"Good morning," she said. "We're just about ready. Come in."

She backed up and he passed close by her, smelling a soft, jasmine perfume. He knew it was jasmine because that had been Meg's favorite, and together they'd planted jasmine bushes along the front porch. In the early mornings they used to sit out, talking quietly and drinking coffee and smelling the jasmine and planning their day.

The smell of jasmine brought that image back every time. But this time as his mind lingered for an instant in the memory, it shifted—Meg faded, and Clint saw himself and Candace.

Jolted by this, Clint silently nudged himself into attention. He succeeded just in time to see Charles round the corner into the living room.

"Hey, Charlie," he said, grinning—and grateful for the distraction from the boy's mother, "looking good."

Charles bristled at the name and opened his mouth to say something snotty. Then, on second thought, he grinned back. "Hey, Clinty," he drawled, "you're not looking so bad yourself."

Clint laughed, and Candace laughed, and then Charles laughed, too. Clint felt so good inside he thought his chest might burst open.

He knew he shouldn't be feeling this way, knew he shouldn't be allowing it. There was a professional distance he should be keeping here, an emotional guard around himself to keep from getting too involved.

He knew how it worked; he'd had to do it with each of the boys.

Yet . . . today was Sunday, the day of rest.

Maybe he'd just let himself enjoy, and work on finding and building that necessary wall within himself tomorrow.

"If you're ready," he said, "we should probably start heading for the church."

"We're ready," Charles said, heading for the door. "*I* was ready ten minutes ago, but Mom messed me up and I had to go back and . . ."

Grinning, Clint listened to the little monster gripe, and he led them out of the house and helped them into the truck. Jasmine filled the cab, and Charles filled the silence. Just for today, Clint couldn't think of anything that could have pleased him more.

Cedar Grove Congregational had a youth pastor with its own youth service, but Charles, of course, opted to sit with the adults.

As they entered the sanctuary, Clint went to his usual spot, near the back and to the left of center aisle.

He spotted Alice near the front, chatting with Glory Swearengen and her cronies. Normally Alice sat with him, out of pity, Clint knew, and he grinned wryly at how quickly she'd switched seats.

Clint introduced his guests to the people in the immediate surrounding pews, and then the choir came out, the music began, and they settled in for the service, Candace on the inside, Charles in the middle and Clint on the aisle.

The sermon was about spring and new growth and new hope, and Clint noticed that Candace listened attentively. He knew she was finding a personal message in Josh Randall's sermon because of the move and her own new beginnings. Even Charles listened to the minister, blond head cocked, eyes narrowed as he evaluated the points Josh made. Clint watched the boy, amazed again at Charles's intelligence and understanding.

After the closing prayer Charles looked at Clint and said simply, "He's a pretty smart guy."

Clint grinned and itched to ruffle Charles's hair, but didn't. "He sure is, sport. Now, how about we go downstairs for some chow?"

"Chow?" Charles queried and rolled his eyes at the term.

"Yeah," Clint said. "You got a problem with that?"

Charles smirked. "I guess not. At least you didn't say *grub*.

Clint put a hand on Charles's back and pushed him out into the aisle. "Get going, Charlie."

"I'm going, Clinty."

Clint looked at Candace. "Jeez, lady. Where did you get this kid?"

The families of the church had combined to provide quite a spread. There were meats and salads and vegetables and breads and about twenty different desserts. After filling their plates, Clint and party found a table near the back of the big basement room, called Fellowship Hall. The room could use a fresh coat of paint, Clint realized, and made a mental note to see if he could get the boys to volunteer to help.

After settling his guests, Clint went back to the buffet to fetch drinks, silverware and napkins.

Charles dug into the food like a man starved.

Clint passed the salt- and pepper shakers to Candace. "So," he said to Charles, "I guess you don't have a problem with chow."

"Guess not," Charles said, between gnaws on a chicken leg. "Did Alice bring this chicken? This is as good as it was yesterday at your house."

"No," Clint said. "And if you're as smart as you think you are, you won't tell Alice it's as good, either."

Charles grinned, bit off more chicken and pushed his glasses up on his nose. "So," he said and spared Clint a quick glance, "how come you're not married, anyway?"

Candace, who had just taken a drink of iced tea, choked. "Charles!"

"What?"

"That was impolite. It's also none of your business."

Clint chuckled and thought if he knew this kid a hundred years, he could still get a kick out of him.

"It's okay," Clint said. "Us horse-riding partners have to know who we're riding with. To answer your question, Charles, I was married for a long time to a very fine lady."

"So you're divorced?" Charles asked, and Candace covered her face with her hands.

She wanted to quiet him on the subject, but Clint had okayed it and left himself wide open. Too, there was a certain curiosity on her own part to hear the answers to questions she wouldn't allow herself to ask.

She was peeking through her fingers when Clint said, "No, I'm not divorced. My wife got sick, Charles. She died. I lost her five years ago."

Candace quit playing games and lowered her hands from her face.

"Oh," Charles said, somber now, too. "Sorry."

"Me, too," Clint said. "But I have to tell you that I've gotten to the point where I can let things be the way they have to be. I do miss her, but I try to just be glad that I had her for the time that I did. You know what I'm saying?"

Charles thought about it, then nodded. "Yeah, I think so. I've sort of been starting to feel that way about my dad."

Candace bit her lower lip and studied her plate. No matter which way you looked at it, the end of a marriage really stank all the way around.

"So," Clint said, leaning back in his folding chair after lunch, "what do you think of our boy?"

Candace looked over to where Charles was making a second trip to the dessert table, craning his neck to see what was there and glancing, too, over at the bake-sale items. There was a chocolate-fudge cake he kept eyeing, and Candace had promised he could buy it as soon as they opened the tables for sale.

"I think," she said, "that our boy is going to weigh three hundred pounds before he's ten."

Clint laughed. "I like to see a kid eat."

"Me, too," Candace admitted, making dents around the rim of her foam coffee cup with a thumb-nail. "His appetite hasn't been good for months. I've been worried about him being so thin."

"I don't think you'll have to worry about that much longer."

"No," Candace said, then met his gaze. "I'm sorry about your wife. I didn't know."

Clint shrugged gently. "Things happen," he said. "But like I told Charles, I really have come to the point where I'm glad to have had the time we had. I was pretty bitter for a while, but now...it's worked itself out."

"I'm glad," she said, and a silence fell. She looked up from her coffee cup and saw him studying her through lazily narrowed eyes. "To answer your question about Charles...I think it's amazing. The change in his whole outlook is...unbelievable."

"A horse'll do that for a kid," Blackwell said, leaning forward now to put his elbows on the table. "There's something about a kid and a horse that—"

"No," Candace said and held his gaze. "It wasn't the horse. It was you."

Clint shifted, suddenly uncomfortable. While her voice was low and sure and steady, there was something in her eyes that communicated an intensity that rocked him.

It wasn't the horse. It was you.

Candace Whitney had a way of making him feel like he could take on the world . . . and win, like Sir Lancelot or something. And maybe it was corny and macho and sexist, but when she looked at him like that, she made him want to go out and slay dragons for her.

"Coyote's a great horse," he said instead, feeling suddenly restless and unsettled by the charge of emotions running through him. "Hey, look. They're opening the bake sale."

He got up, breaking both the mood and the tension and feeling so much better for it.

He wiped his hand across his mouth, because sweat had popped out on his upper lip and started to bead.

Something was happening here, something he hadn't expected to happen to him again in his lifetime. Something, too, he wasn't at all sure he wanted. There something new in these feelings, yes. New and exciting. But there was familiarity, too, and he knew where these schizoid images and emotions could lead.

To heaven and to heartache.

To the heights and the depths.

Just thinking about the possibilities made his blood heat . . . and then freeze.

"Clint!" a male voice said, and then Josh Randall, the minister and kid brother of an old schoolmate of Clint's, clapped him on the back. "I'm glad to see you brought a guest," Josh said, smiling over at Candace and offering her his hand.

"Candace Whitney," Clint said, making the obligatory introductions, "Josh Randall, our pastor. And over there with that huge chocolate cake is her son, Charles."

"Ah," Josh said, grinning at the little boy with the big cake. "You'll have to introduce me to him, too."

Clint made the mistake of catching Candace's eye, and they shared a moment of hesitation that was followed by amusement, both of them not quite sure what to expect of Charles. They laughed, and Josh Randall looked at them, eyebrows raised.

"I said something funny?"

"Not at all," Clint said. "Come on, Brother. I'll be happy to introduce you to Charles."

When the minister turned and moved toward Charles, Candace, behind him, put her hand to her forehead, wincing in dread. Clint put a hand on the small of her back and, laughing, guided her over to her son.

Chapter Six

"I noticed you during the service," Josh Randall said to Charles, after meeting him without a hitch. "You seemed to be listening very closely. What did you think?"

Charles pushed his glasses up on his nose, frowning in thought. "Well, I think you might have had a point about new beginnings, and about the way trees and grass seem to die for the winter, but it's really only a new stage because they start growing again in the spring. I mean, I think maybe that *is* what people do sometimes, too."

"Oh," Josh Randall said, staring at Charles.

Clint grinned, and felt like sticking out his chest and hitching his thumbs in his belt loops with pride.

"Well," Josh said, "I'm glad you think so, Charles." He glanced at Clint and Candace, who only smiled innocently in return.

"Still," Charles said, "I'm not that sure about what you said about some of that other stuff."

"Oh?" Josh said. "Like what?"

Charles shrugged. "Well, like God guiding our footsteps and telling us which road to take. I mean, what does He do? Just call down from Heaven and say, 'Hey, you! Do this!' And another thing I didn't get was when—"

Josh Randall held up a finger. "Excuse me for one second, Charles."

"Sure," Charles said.

"Mrs. Whitney," Josh said, "would you mind if I borrowed your son for a few minutes? This promises to be one of the most challenging and interesting theological discussions I've had in a long time."

"Be my guest," Candace said, feeling very proud of her bright and handsome son.

"Let's go sit down," Randall said to Charles.

"Okay."

"Hey, Brother," Randall said to Clint. "While we're gone, you ought to introduce Mrs. Whitney to some of the other young mothers."

"Will do," Clint said.

As the minister started to guide Charles toward a table, Charles paused and looked up at Clint, gesturing to the pastor with a thumb. "This guy's your brother, Clint?"

Clint laughed. "In a manner of speaking."

"Come on and sit down, Charles," Josh said. "I'll try to clear that one up for you, too."

Clint and Candace watched the pair move off, and Candace sighed, contented that Charles did not seem interested in being rude and insulting—only challenging and questioning, things she wanted him always to be. She liked that he knew how to think and evaluate and judge for himself, even at six years old. Candace knew grown-ups who couldn't do that.

"He's a great kid," Clint said, still watching after him.

"Yes," Candace said, pleased that other people were finally getting a chance to see this. "He really is."

"Well," Clint said, pulling his thoughts back from Charles and looking around, "what do you say, Mrs. Whitney? Are you ready to plunge into the social whirl of Cedar Grove?"

"Why not?" Candace replied, and as Clint picked out a group of people for her to meet, Candace took far too much pleasure in the presence of him next to her—*and* in the warm pressure of his hand on the small of her back as he guided her around.

Dear Dad,

Sorry I haven't written for a few days, but I've been really busy.

Last Sunday, Clint (Clint Blackwell, with the ranch) invited us to his church and this dinner thing after. That was fun and we bought a ton of pies and cakes and cookies from their bake sale.

School's going okay, and there's this one kid (Tommy Blake) who's interested in computers, too. He doesn't know much about them, but he came over the other night and I showed him some stuff on mine. Thanks for the scanner you sent. It's pretty rad. I tried to call you when I got it, but your new housekeeper was there, and she said you and Gina went to Vail for a few days. I guess you wouldn't really want to spend your vacation time in Cedar Grove. There's really not that much to do.

I've been riding Coyote (the horse I told you about) almost every day after school. Clint says I'm getting to be pretty good at it, almost like a regular cowboy. I never thought I'd like getting called a cowboy, but I kinda do. The other day Clint gave me a cowboy hat—a real felt Stetson. We got goofy then and started acting like Clint Eastwood and John Wayne. He's been calling me Pilgrim ever since, but I guess that's okay. He calls Mom 'Ma'am' now and she thinks he's a real nut. He is pretty funny, and I haven't seen Mom laugh so much in a long time.

Anyway, sorry again that I haven't been writing so often, but I know you know how it is to be busy. If you get a chance, call or write, and I'll write again in a couple days.

Hope you had a good trip to Vail, and take care.

Your son,
Charles

Things were going well—her life in general and the progress with Charles and outlook for the future in particular. Candace found herself smiling and humming her way through her workday—and looking forward to what had become their routine over the last couple of weeks, going out to the Double C.

Every day after school, Clint and Charles went riding. They'd taken to inviting Candace along, but thus far she'd held back, not wanting her presence to hinder the progress. She spent that hour drinking coffee with Alice or helping shell peas or peel potatoes for dinner. Usually Candace and Charles left right after the ride, but once in a while they would accept Clint and Alice's invitation to stay.

Like tonight. It was Friday night, and she and Alice were going to cook up a big batch of enchiladas.

"What are you grinning about?" Jack Harden said, stopping at her desk.

Candace shrugged. "I don't know. I just feel like it, I guess."

"It's Friday," Jack said, wiggling his eyebrows. "My guess would be that the lady has a date."

Candace pulled her purse and briefcase from the bottom desk drawer. "Your guess would be wrong," she said. "I'm going to spend my Friday night teaching a woman friend how to do Mexican food California-style.''

Jack rolled his eyes and straightened from her desk. "Boy, you big-city types really know how to live."

No, Candace thought, getting up from her desk. But I'm learning, Jack. I'm definitely learning....

"Now *this* is great," Clint said, after his first bite of the spicy enchilada.

"It really is," Alice said. "And the rest of the stuff is good, too."

They'd done it up right, making fresh guacamole, shredded lettuce and tomato salads, spicy fried rice. Candace just sat back and grinned, glad to be able to return some of the good cooking and hospitality she'd received at the ranch.

"Hey, Pilgrim," Clint said to Charles, "I thought you told me your mom couldn't cook?"

Candace raised an eyebrow and looked at her son. On the chair next to him was his tan felt Stetson, four-star, an expensive gift from Clint. While they'd all insisted he not wear the hat at the table, nobody had the heart to tell him he couldn't keep it next to him.

"I never said she *couldn't* cook," Charles said, sticking up for himself under Candace's look. "I said she *didn't* cook."

"Charles!" Candace said, because she'd been cooking dinner every night since they'd made this move. Before, back home, she'd been so pushed for time, and all of their schedules had been so hectic and unpredictable, she'd ordered in a lot or pulled something out of the freezer. But now...

"Well, you didn't," Charles said, blinking innocently. "Not until we moved here. I was just telling Clint that I didn't know if dinner tonight was going to be any good or not, because I didn't even know you knew how to make enchiladas."

"Well," Candace said, "I guess I haven't made them for a long time."

The fact was, she suddenly realized, that she hadn't cooked her favorite Mexican dishes in years because they were the things she and Eric had done together, back in the beginning, back in the good times. She didn't know when she'd quit fixing them, but looking back, she supposed it stopped happening when everything else they'd done together fell apart.

Funny she hadn't thought about that at all when planning or shopping or preparing this dinner. Funny how she'd only had one thought in mind when Clint and Alice mentioned they ought to have some tacos or something one of these days.

Funny how all she'd thought about since then was that this was a way she could please two people who had done so much for her and her son.

"Anyway," Charles said, pushing his glasses up and looking at her earnestly, "they're really good, Mom."

"Thank you, Charles."

"You're welcome. Are we really going to have fried ice cream for dessert?"

Candace smiled. "We really are, so save room."

"No problem," Charles said, tucking into the mound of food on his plate. "Come on, Clint, let's eat."

"I'm working on it, Pilgrim," Clint drawled. "But keeping up with you is a tall order."

Charles grinned and drank some milk. "I know. But a kid needs energy to keep going. When I get to be your age, I guess I'll have to watch it, too. I hear when you get old, it all goes to fat."

Candace started to say something, then didn't, realizing that Clint and her son had indeed come to their own understanding. This teasing between them went on eternally, and both parties seemed to enjoy it.

Clint took a long drink of his iced tea, then looked at Charles before answering. "When you get old, it all goes to fat," he said casually. "But when you're a six-year-old rug rat, it apparently all goes to mouth."

At which point he reached over and poked Charles in the ribs. Charles lurched sideways to avoid it, then poked Clint in the stomach to retaliate.

"Boys!" Alice said sharply, but of course this had no effect. She turned to Candace, her mouth slanting wryly. "You thought it was bad with one of them. Now we've got two."

"Mmm," Candace agreed. Propping her chin on one hand, she worked hard to hide the profound pleasure she got from watching her son engage in this ridiculous and ill-mannered horseplay with the handsome and ornery rancher who threw teenage boys in watering troughs, called her son Pilgrim, and winked at her and called her Ma'am.

"That was some mighty fine chow, ladies," Clint said after the ice cream and coffee, leaning back in his chair and rubbing his full stomach—*and* doing the exaggerated cowboy routine he and Charles liked to fall into twenty times a day.

"Why, thank you, kind sir," Candace said, getting up to clear.

"You just sit yourself right down, Ma'am." Clint rose. "Me and the little cowpoke here are doing dishes tonight."

"We are?" Charles said, frowning.

"We are," Clint said dryly. "These ladies cook us up a fine meal like this, I think it's only the gentlemanly thing to do, don't you?"

Charles clearly didn't want to think about this subject at all, but reluctantly conceded. "All right," he grumbled, dragging himself to his feet. "But I thought we could play video games tonight. I brought my Nintendo and—"

"Video games?" Clint scowled, carrying guacamole and chips to the kitchen. "I don't play video games."

"You could learn," Charles said. "Even old dogs can learn new tricks."

Clint cast a look over his shoulder at Candace. She shrugged, grinned and waited to see how he got out of this one.

"I tried horseback riding when I didn't want to," Charles said, stowing salsa in the fridge. "And I tried roping and jumping and even mucking out stalls!"

"All right," Clint said, holding up his hands in surrender. "All right. I'll try it, I'll try it. But I'm going to go about it like you do, hotshot. I'll try it, but I'm not going to like it."

"That isn't the way to do it," Charles said. "You can't judge something before you even . . ." Then, finally registering the first part of Clint's statement, he trailed off sheepishly.

"It's not?" Clint asked, all innocence. "You mean a person ought to try all kinds of things before he decides what he likes and doesn't like?"

"Maybe," Charles said, sticking his small nose in the air. "Boy, you really think you're Freud or somebody, don't you?"

Clint laughed and shook his head. "Charlie, Charlie, Charlie," he said. "What are we going to do with you?"

In the end they all helped with the clearing and dishes, and the kitchen was back in order in minutes. Amused, Candace and Alice followed Charles and Clint into the living room and sat back to watch Clint get his orientation into the world of electronic stress and pressure.

"You call this fun?" Clint said, when Charles had blown up Clint's space patrol for the third time. "This isn't fun. This is work."

"No," Charles said. "It's kind of like riding a horse, Clinty. It's not work. It's a pleasure."

Clint messed up Charles's hair, and Charles rolled back on the floor, cackling. "Come on," he said, when he'd sat back up in front of the TV. "This time I'll go easy on you."

"Forget that," Clint said, trying to get more comfortable on the floor. "I don't need your charity."

But after another hour the tally remained the same: Charles all, Clint nothing.

"That's enough for me," Clint said, shoving the hand control aside. Charles protested, but Clint was firm. "We'll play again another time, Charlie. Right now, though, I'm wondering if I can unbend enough to get up off the floor."

He'd been sitting cross-legged, like Charles, and his knees had gone stiff. They cracked as he straightened them, and he wondered how long it had been since he'd sat that way for any length of time. Getting old, Blackwell, his mind jeered. Just like days when he spent too much time in the saddle. He felt about twenty-five most of the time, but the fact was he was beating forty on the back, and every once in a while, like now, he was sharply reminded.

Time was passing, getting away. Why was it that just lately, over the past few weeks, he kept being hit by the sense that life, if he wasn't very careful, was going to pass him by?

"Need a hand, Clinty?" Charles taunted, having scrambled to his feet in seconds.

Clint looked at the boy, standing there holding out his hand to help him up.

I want this kid, he thought, and the thought and its possessiveness shocked him. I want him here more than an hour or two a day. I want to teach him things and watch him grow and beat him at Space Patrol on Friday nights and cook him big ranch house breakfasts on Saturday mornings.

He looked over at Candace, smiling at the two of them from her place by Alice on the couch.

And his stomach turned over.

She belongs here, he thought. Charles belongs here, and Candace belongs here, and . . . I love her.

"Let's watch a movie," Charles said, trying to pull Clint to his feet.

"I have an idea," Alice said. "Why don't we do something nonelectronic."

"Good idea," Candace said.

"Like what?" Charles frowned. "It's dark out, so we can't go riding or anything."

"Still," Candace said, "there are other things to do besides play with machines. Alice, what did you have in mind?"

"Well, we could play cards," Alice said. "Or maybe we could talk Clint into getting out his guitar."

"You play?" Candace said, liking the idea.

"Not really," Clint said, standing in the middle of the room, his home, yet feeling vaguely disoriented.

"He plays beautifully," Alice said. "And he has a very nice singing voice, too."

Alice got up to get the guitar, and Clint was left looking at Candace and Charles—and realizing he had done the unforgivable. He had failed to build walls around his personal feelings and deliberately not thought about it much since the very beginning.

It had been so great having the two of them around. He'd found it so easy to just go with the flow and enjoy them. And now . . . ?

Now it was too late. He was involved. He was more than involved.

"Will you play for us?" Candace asked.

I'd do anything you asked me to, Clint thought.

"Sure," he said. "But only if everybody else will sing along." They sang "Oh, Susannah!" and "Red River Valley" and "The Yellow Rose of Texas."

They sang gospel songs and country tunes, and Candace couldn't remember ever having had a better time in her life.

Eventually Charles began to slump in his corner of the couch, the long day catching up to him. Soon, lulled by the music and his full belly, he drifted off to sleep.

Seeing this, the grown-ups, smiling, let the volume and tempo of their music die down and quietly slipped out of the living room and back to the kitchen, where Alice made fresh coffee.

"Just one cup," Candace said, knowing she should be taking herself and her son home, but loath to end the evening. It had been so . . . complete. So complete, in fact, that it was one of those things she didn't want to think about too much, lest the significance force her to take some action she didn't want to take. Like, for instance, spend less time here. Or...

But no. The moment was too good to spoil with intelligent thought.

Alice brought coffee to the kitchen table—but only two cups.

"Where's yours?" Candace said.

Alice shook her head. "I don't drink coffee after nine at night. I'd be up till two. Actually—" a yawn broke her sentence in half "—I think I'm going to head off to bed."

"Good night," Clint said, watching her with a lazy smile.

"It's ten o'clock," Candace realized, looking at her watch after Alice left the room. "I didn't realize it was getting so late."

"Tomorrow's Saturday," Clint said. "You don't have to go to work. Charles doesn't have to get up for school. Stay awhile."

"I... all right."

It was all the persuasion she needed, and as the house grew silent, Charles sleeping in the other room and Alice at the far end of the house preparing for bed, Candace felt that she could stay here more than a while. She could stay... maybe a lifetime.

"This is a great house," she said, to get her thoughts off that other, dangerous track.

"I like it," Clint said, leaning back in his chair, one long leg propped on the other under the table. "My grandparents built it. It's almost a hundred years old. Except for college and my tour in Nam, I've spent most of my life in this place.''

And he guessed he'd probably die here, too. That didn't bother him. What had begun to bother him, just lately, was the idea of living and dying here alone.

Before, after Meg, he'd always felt he'd had the best and was grateful to have had it. And that anything else—*anyone* else—would be nothing but a shallow substitute. He'd wanted kids, kids of his own, but had settled for his work with the boys, because marrying for kids was something he couldn't and wouldn't do.

But now...

Life, the future, without Candace and Charles seemed ... empty. Nearly pointless.

How had this happened so completely and overwhelmingly?

And how, *how* could he have let it?

Yet he hadn't even tried to stop it. He loved them, both of them, and knew enough about his own feelings to know how deep they ran. Yet what did it mean in terms of the future—or even the present?

In short, he loved them overpoweringly and needed them in his life.

But this was supposed to be a business arrangement. Nothing romantic or very personal had transpired or even been alluded to between him and Candace in all these weeks. Business, just so. And while Candace was obviously very happy with the outcome of their arrangement, did her feelings stop there? And when the business of helping Charles was done, where did that leave him?

It was a question that thrummed at him, almost panicked him and felt like a big fist squeezing at his stomach. Lord. He'd come through Vietnam only to lose Meg and had had to battle to learn to care about life enough to go on. He wondered if he'd have the strength or fortitude to go into that battle again.

"The Double C," Candace said. "What does that stand for?"

"Uh," Clint said, dragging his thoughts back to the present. "Clint and Cecille."

"Your grandparents."

"Mmm-hmm." Then, suddenly restless, Clint sat forward. "It's a beautiful night out tonight. You want to take our coffee outside?"

"Sure," she said, and rose with slim grace.

She wasn't like Meg, Clint thought, his gaze running over her. Meg had been small and dark haired and dark eyed. Candace was tall and willowy and golden. But both women shared qualities that drew him—intelligence, a sense of humor.

Candace challenged and intrigued him in different ways than Meg had, but just as strongly. Both times in his life, the memory of the woman had lingered and tickled at his mind from the very first meeting.

And the chemistry...

Again, different with each, but in both cases the chemistry had a rare power.

"Come on," he said, and, carrying his coffee mug in one hand, did nothing to fight the urge to put a hand on her waist to guide her to the door.

He was probably going to hurt over this whole situation.

Probably, nearly certainly.

But not tonight.

For tonight the new and sure and exciting and frightening knowledge that he could really love again after Meg made him feel scared. But more than that, it made him feel young and alive and hopeful again. Made him feel . . . reborn.

Chapter Seven

An old wooden glider sat on the wide wooden porch, facing the corral and outbuildings. Beyond them, green pasture nestled between two gently rolling hills.

It was dark, of course, but Candace knew the view well by now, knew how peaceful and clean it looked at morning and midday; knew how mellow and golden it looked at sunset. She didn't know how it looked out here at sunrise and found herself imagining everything all silvery and dew dampened and early-morning misty.

They sat on the glider, side by side, not touching but almost, and she felt the warmth of him down her whole left side, even through her sweater and jeans.

"Warm enough?" Clint asked, because they hadn't bothered to put on jackets.

Candace nodded, glad for the darkness, because she could feel herself flushing at his innocuous question, which had followed directly her own awareness of his body heat.

"It's a beautiful night," she said and sipped at her coffee.

It was the third week in May. She'd known Clint Blackwell almost six weeks.

They spent a few minutes in silence. Neither of them fought it. Candace thought if she lived to be a hundred, she might never have a more perfect evening. There was a sense of absolute contentment that astounded her.

Eventually Clint set his empty cup on the table next to him, and the glider began to creak as they rocked. Candace got rid of her cup, too, and pulled her legs up to sit cross-legged while Clint made the glider sway.

"So," he asked, "how are things—in general, I mean?"

"Things are great," Candace said and meant it. She couldn't remember her life feeling so right in years. Maybe ever. Before, she'd had challenge and accomplishment and excitement and activity. Now, though, she had peace; and for her, for now, nothing could have felt better.

"How about you?" she asked, turning to study his profile. "How are things—in general?"

"They're good," Clint said, nodding. "Real good."

"That's good," Candace said and frowned a little at the awkwardness that was beginning to creep up between them. She wondered at it, rebelled at the very idea of it, then realized why it had come. In all these weeks of being together and getting to know each other, she and Clint Blackwell had never spent more than five minutes together alone.

That didn't seem possible, but in retrospect, she realized it was so. During all their time Charles or Alice had been there as buffers. Now, alone, she was becoming more conscious of his presence by the second. And more self-conscious, too.

She didn't like this, not at all. She wanted to go right back to where being together was right and easy. She wanted, she realized, to have Alice or Charles here, because then she could go back to being safe.

This one-on-one business was both dangerous and scary. Becoming more and more conscious of his closeness, she was hit anew with the reactions and sensations that made her feel he was just possibly the most attractive, sexiest man she'd ever met in her life.

"I guess I really should be going," she said, when the tension within her grew to be unbearable.

For a long second she thought Clint, lost in his own thoughts, hadn't heard her at all. Then he turned to her and she felt caught by his gaze.

"Don't," he said, and then he was moving closer, and her heart started to pound because she knew, and the warmth she'd felt earlier turned into heat, and his hand touched her cheek, and his mouth found hers. And her senses, already rocking, exploded.

It was one kiss. Just one kiss and no more, and then Clint drew back and continued to rock the glider and they sat there on the porch in silence for what felt like an eternity.

Candace knew she should leave, but she wanted to move back into his arms. So she did neither, instead opting just to sit and and rock and listen to the creaking and squeaking of the swing and the loud and scary yet thrilling pounding of her heart.

"Maybe we should go inside," Clint said at last, still looking straight ahead, profile outlined by the glow of the moon.

"Yes," Candace said, voice husky. "Maybe we should."

"So why'd you let me stay asleep last night?" Charles demanded first thing the next morning.

Candace went to the refrigerator to gather pancake fixings. "Because you were tired, Charles. If you weren't, you wouldn't have fallen asleep in the first place."

"I could have woken up," Charles said, pulling out his chair at the kitchen table. "So what'd you guys do? What'd I miss out on?"

Candace avoided his look and dumped dry pancake mix into a mixing bowl. "Nothing, Charles. We talked."

"What about?" Charles said. "Me?"

"Actually, no," Candace realized. For probably the first time, she and Clint Blackwell hadn't discussed her son at all. "We just talked about . . . things."

And not many things at that.

Still, she'd spent the night realizing that their few minutes alone had resulted in a whole world of communication.

After their time on the porch, she knew things about herself and about Clint Blackwell that she wasn't entirely sure she wanted to know. Like this hero-crush thing she'd been battling from the start. Last night she'd realized it was more than what Morgan had felt for her sixty-year-old divorce lawyer. And whatever it was, it wasn't a mere crush, and it wasn't going to wear off.

Learning that Clint Blackwell did in fact return her feelings of attraction made things either more complicated or more simple. Trouble was, Candace couldn't decide which. She felt confused and elated and hot and cold. She felt excited and thrilled and anxious to see him again—and wondered how she could arrange things so she wouldn't have to.

Shaking her head at her own flakiness, she tried to quit analyzing it all and poured Charles some orange juice.

"Thanks," he said as she set it on the table in front of him.

"You're welcome."

"You know," Charles said casually, "I thought you two might have been talking about how well your little plan worked."

At the counter by the sink, Candace paused in mixing the pancake batter. "Our little plan? Charles, what are you talking about?"

"You know," he said and shrugged. "Yours and Clint's plan to make me like Cedar Grove. It's worked pretty good, so I figure that's what you talked about."

"No," Candace said cautiously. "And I don't know that you would exactly call it a plan. Clint just knew you weren't happy, and he wanted to help."

"It was a setup," Charles said. "But I don't mind. Because me and Clint are past all that. It's not like when he works with the kids in trouble anymore. Me and Clint are friends."

"You are?" Candace asked, not knowing what else to say. She was stunned at the full grasp Charles had of the whole situation. The child was six years old, for Pete's sake. Why couldn't he ever take *anything* at face value?

"Sure," Charles said. "Clint doesn't think of me as a job anymore. Like with the delinquents he—"

"Charles, I really don't think you should call those boys that."

"Why?" Charles said. "Clint does."

"Clint is a grown-up. Besides, he's just teasing. That's sort of an affectionate term for the boys."

"I *know* that," Charles said, rolling his eyes. "That's why *I* call them that. They don't get offended. I don't get offended when they call me city boy, either. Or Einstein or hotshot or rug rat. Or when they try to get me to do something by telling me not to be such a weenie.''

''They call you a weenie?''

''That's what we do, Mom. You know, it's a guy thing.''

''I see,'' Candace said and poured the first half cup of pancake batter into hot oil.

A guy thing. Her six-year-old son trading insults with a bunch of hardcase teenagers and a rancher. When stated like that, it hardly seemed the ideal situation. But watching Charles, she knew he'd found something he'd never really had—a relationship with a father figure and a passel of boys who treated him with the affectionate disdain you'd get from older brothers.

Charles's relationship with Eric had never been the teasing, razzing, wrestling kind of thing he had going with Clint. Eric, she realized now, had always kept Charles at a distance. He was his son, yes. But Eric had created something of an owner-object sort of situation with Charles rather than a relationship.

He was proud of Charles and spent the money and made the arrangements that supported Eric's ideals. He dressed him well and sent him to the right schools. He opened bank accounts and started a stock portfolio and taught him how to follow the market so he could brag about his son to his friends. But beyond that, nothing.

Beyond that, he hadn't the interest or time. Charles, Candace realized, had not been Eric's life. He'd been like a cute, bright accessory to his life, and that was it. An accessory or a pet. Something to show off when convenient and put away or ignore when not.

Why hadn't she seen that at the time? Now, in retrospect, it all seemed so clear, but then...

Then she hadn't had anything with which to compare a good father-son relationship.

Now, after only six weeks, seeing Charles and Clint together gave her a definite sense of what fathers and sons should be all about.

She flipped the pancake over and listened to the wet side sizzle.

It's a guy thing.

Okay. Terrific. And she was very, very grateful that her son had found this.

But what about this thing that was happening between *herself* and Clint?

What was it exactly, and what did it mean?

Mere physical attraction, strong but shallow?

Friendship growing daily into something... deeper and stronger?

Last night on the porch, Clint had made the decision to change things between them completely. And she had made the decision to go right along and change them, as well.

But what did it actually *mean* as of now?

And if what Charles had going at the Double C was a "guy thing," what did that make what *she* had going?

She guessed she knew.

What had been successively a "work thing," then a "friend thing," had suddenly become by mutual consent a "man-woman thing."

A man-woman thing with a child who might get caught in the middle if it didn't work out. A man-woman thing that really had no future because when she thought about it realistically, she knew she couldn't jeopardize what Charles had with Clint for anything. She owed it to her son to let his relationship with Clint Blackwell grow and to keep hers light and simple. Friendly, but not overly so.

The pancake was golden brown. She flipped it onto a plate and set it in front of Charles.

"Here you go, sweetie," she said.

I'm sorry, she thought. *I'm sorry for last night and taking any chance complicating or endangering the happiness you've finally found.*

She *was* sorry, for both herself and Charles. And as she poured out more batter into the skillet, she promised herself that for her son's sake, she wouldn't let anything like last night happen again.

It was Saturday, and on Saturdays Charles liked to spend the whole day out at the Double C. The older boys were there all day, too, and while the male delegation worked the ranch and tended the stock, Candace and Alice had started making Saturdays baking days. This Saturday they were supposed to be baking bread, but Candace kept trying to think of a way to stay clear of the ranch.

"Come *on,* Mom," Charles said, dressed and ready to go. His jeans were wearing at the knees and seat, his boots were scuffed and broken in, and his hat, his prize Stetson from Clint, was on his head.

"I'm coming," Candace said, dragging her feet.

After last night, how was she supposed to act?

"You know, Charles, I think I heard something about rain for today. Maybe we should stay home and take care of some things around here."

"It's not going to rain," Charles said. "Besides, what if it does? You still have to take care of business. The animals don't feed and water themselves, you know. So if it rains, Clint's going to need my help even more. But it's not going to rain."

He was, of course, correct. It was a gorgeous May day, already warm and destined to get almost hot. Candace wore a painted T-shirt and jeans and a pair of white canvas sneakers. She'd pulled her hair back in a ponytail and felt about twelve—in more ways than one. Just the thought of seeing Clint again after last night made her feel giddy and nervous and almost adolescently nauseated. She remembered one friend from junior high who had had to throw up before every date with her football-player boyfriend.

Back then Candace had never been quite *that* nervous. But today...

"Mo-om!" Charles whined. "Come on!"

"Hey, Clint?" Ian said, coming from the bright sunshine into the dim, horsey coolness of the barn.

Clint paused in front of Coyote's box stall, pitchfork in hand, and straightened to look at slim, dark-haired Ian.

"Me and the guys were wondering if maybe we could knock off a little early today—say around three-thirty."

Clint frowned. "*All* of you? Why?"

Ian shrugged and stuck his hands into the front pockets of his ancient, torn jeans. "We were sort of hoping to get in an extra hour or two of warming up before the practice game tonight."

Clint's frown smoothed out. "Ah. Losing the other night kind of stuck in your craw, did it?"

"Drake's team is tough," Ian said. "Tomorrow, when the real games start, we want to be ready."

Clint stuck the pitchfork into the cut bale of fresh straw and tossed some into Coyote's empty stall. The horses were out today, enjoying the weather, and Clint knew that's where he ought to be. He could be doing the barn work anytime. But he'd come here as he often did when he needed to be alone and think. Something about the barn, with its dimness and smells of horse and hay and saddle soap and old leather, soothed him, quieted his mind.

"You know why you guys lost that practice game to Pete's team, don't you?" Clint said and continued to pitch the straw.

Ian shifted, shuffling at a patch of grain dust on the concrete floor. "No," he lied. "I guess they're just better."

"Wrong," Clint said, still working steadily. "You lost because the four of you quit playing as a team. Bobby, Dean and Ray had Pete Drake as a principal a few years ago, and instead of playing a good, competitive game for fun, you guys turned it into a grudge game—the hoods against the teacher. Ray completely ignored my signals when he was pitching to Pete, and Pete got three runs off him."

"But we didn't—"

"Bull."

"Okay," Ian said reluctantly. "I guess we did."

Clint set his pitchfork against the wall. "I guess you did. And before you play Peter Drake's team tomorrow, I suggest you get your attitudes together. Adults aren't your enemy, Ian. And on a church softball team, there's no principal and no student. You're all equals. If you forget about trying to be a tough guy and play for the sport, you'll have a whole lot more fun."

Ian, chastised, looked at the ground for a long second, then turned to leave. Clint sighed and leaned back against the box stall. He'd been meaning to talk to the guys about their attitudes, but he hadn't meant to do it quite this way. Now it was done, Ian felt like an idiot, and Clint would have to deal with fixing that situation now on top of the authority problem the boys had in the first place.

Great.

Like last night.

On the porch.

Then, too, he'd acted impulsively and complicated a situation that was already not simple.

He shook his head, pushed himself away from the wall and went after Ian. Best to talk to the boys and get things straightened out now rather than let any bruised feelings linger.

As he rounded the corral, he saw Candace's BMW cruise up to the house, Charles waving his Stetson out the window.

He sketched them a wave, then headed for the boys. First them, then the stickier question of how Candace was feeling about him today and how things were going to be between them from now on.

"Well, if you want my opinion," Charles was saying, perched next to Bobby on the top rail of the corral, "Mr. Drake and Mrs. Dale ought to just quit messing around about it and get married. I mean, *everybody* knows they're goofy for each other."

"Or just plain goofy," Dean murmured, and Clint shot him a silencing look. The boys were pretty careful around Charles. It was one thing to be a tough guy when you were just a few years short of being a grown man. It was quite another thing when you were six going on forty.

So no matter how much Charles seemed to know and understand, Clint had told the older boys at the outset to keep his age and innocence in mind. They knew they could talk to Clint about anything. But in front of Charles, they watched it pretty well.

"Okay, you guys," Clint said, "take off. We can quit work and go practice around three-thirty, but we've got a lot to do between now and then."

He watched them head for their individual chores, then climbed up on the corral rail to sit next to Charles. Clint took off his hat, wiped sweat from his brow and sat slouched, holding his hat in both hands.

"So you think Mr. Drake and Mrs. Dale ought to get married," Clint said, wanting to follow up Charles's thoughts on the subject for his own reasons.

"Sure," Charles said. "They like each other and everybody knows it, so why not?"

Clint shrugged. "Who knows? Maybe they will get married. Or...maybe it's not that simple."

"What's not simple?"

"I don't know," Clint said. "I mean maybe they don't really like each other *that* way. Maybe they're just good friends. Or maybe they wouldn't get along if they were around each other all the time. Or... maybe they have kids or something that wouldn't like it if they married someone else."

Charles frowned. "I never thought about that. You think Mrs. Dale has kids?"

Clint shrugged. Frieda Dale did, in fact, have two teenagers, a boy and a girl, but he didn't want to get sidetracked into that.

"What I'm saying is," Clint said, "even if two grown-ups really cared about each other and wanted to get married, they'd have to think about the kids first, make sure they'd be happy about the whole thing. You know what I mean?"

Charles's eyes narrowed, then he squinted up at Clint, a frown creasing his hat-shaded face. "Yeah," he said. "I think I do know what you mean."

Then, too late, Clint remembered who he was talking to and tried to fix it. "Of course, I don't know anything about it. I mean, maybe they're not married yet for a lot of other reasons. Or maybe..."

But he let the sentence trail off. Charles wasn't listening, anyway. He was frowning slightly, lost in his thoughts, his little computer-like mind figuring things according to new data.

Yeah, Clinty. I think I know what you mean. I think I know exactly what you mean....

"Well, it's about time," Alice said when Clint and Charles came in half an hour late for lunch. "And where are the boys? We made enough ham sandwiches for half the town."

"I told them I'd bring them some lunch when I go back out," Clint said, taking off his muddy boots at the door. "They were going to skip lunch so they can get done early enough to get some extra ball practice in before tonight's practice game. They didn't like losing last week."

"Mmm," Alice said and began to stick sandwiches into plastic bags.

Candace, avoiding looking at Clint directly, went to see if she could help Charles off with his boots.

"I've got it, Mom," Charles said, rolling his eyes. "Jeez, I'm not a baby."

Clint chuckled, and Candace thought he was trying to avoid her look, too. She also wondered if maybe they were late for lunch because he wanted to delay this first-time-after-the-porch meeting as much as she did.

Lord, one kiss.

She was thirty-four years old, had been married for fourteen years, and she was completely scattered over one little kiss!

Get a grip, Candace, Eric told her again. *You're regressing.* And, she told herself, you're acting like a twit!

She forced herself to meet Clint's eyes. "Hello," she said. "I was beginning to think you two had gotten lost somewhere out on the range."

"Not lost," Clint said, and they fell into step beside each other and walked toward the kitchen. "Just delayed. We were out mending fence and wanted to finish up before riding back." He cast her a sideways glance. "Miss us?"

Her stomach flopped. "No," she said airily. "We just didn't want the lunch to go bad."

"You know," Clint said after lunch and over coffee, which he'd insisted they take out onto the dreaded porch. He'd sent Charles to take lunch to the older boys, then to the barn to groom Coyote, and Alice had shooed them both out of the kitchen. And now, here they were, back on the glider, swaying squeakily, both staring straight ahead, the two of them together again, alone. "I've been thinking we should probably talk about last night."

"Uh," Candace said, caught completely off guard by this direct approach. All during lunch she'd begun to feel more at ease, as if that one little kiss really was just one little kiss, not worth feeling awkward about, not worth getting excited about, not worth trying to plan or plot or foresee the future around.

With Charles and Alice there as buffers, things had gone right back to being very normal and very...nice. They were almost like a family when they were all together. But when she and Clint were alone...it didn't feel nice and comfortable and familylike at all.

Like right now. It felt downright nerve jangling. A man-woman thing, no question about it.

"Last night," Candace said, trying to keep her voice light. "Yes, I think we probably should talk about it. The thing is—"

"The thing is, I should probably apologize," Clint said, still looking straight ahead, as was Candace.

They could have been discussing anything, their voices low and even and nonemotional. Candace wondered if her courtroom experience was also keeping the inner commotion out of her face.

"There's no need to apologize," Candace said. "I mean, it wasn't a big deal. It was a gorgeous spring night, the moon was out. The jasmine smelled heavenly." She shrugged and cast a glance his way. "It was a romantic kind of night. Those things just sort of... happen on nights like that, don't you think?"

"I *think,*" Clint said, then stopped himself, frowning a little, his gaze absently fixed on the distant barn. "I think," he said again, quietly, but with new firmness and decision, "it would be a whole lot simpler for me if I could put it down to that."

Then abruptly he rose, and the glider jerked unevenly without his weight to balance the other side. He stood looking down at her, and the hard and determined light in his eyes made her mouth go dry.

"As it is," he said, "I still think I should probably apologize. Because for me, Candace, last night meant a little more than moonlight and romance. I've wanted to kiss you for weeks, so I did. But what I should be apologizing for is starting something I don't want to stop."

With that, he gave her a wry and lopsided smile, fixed his Stetson on his head and tapped the brim. "See you later, pretty lady. I'd better go make sure Charles hasn't tried to reorganize the barn—or unionize the help."

And then he was walking away and Candace was sitting, blinking, staring after him. Feeling what...? Stunned, mainly. Stunned by his candor—*and* by his simple declaration of his desire and intention to let this sort of... *thing* go on.

And then, too, another thing came to her as she watched him disappear inside the barn. Clint Blackwell had not actually apologized for changing things between them at all. No, she realized. He had said he *should* apologize.

And maybe being a lawyer made her naturally picky and oversensitive to distinctions in choice of phrase, but she didn't think so. Everything about Clint's declarations told her there was a vast difference between I *should* regret the turn things have taken, and I *do*.

Chapter Eight

There was no getting out of going to church that Sunday—or to the big game that came after. Though Candace tried a whole list of excuses that seemed perfectly reasonable to her, Charles finally put a stop to it by telling her that Sunday was the Sabbath and did she really think God was asking too much to expect them to give Him one day a week?

Besides, the big game was after, and he'd been helping Clint train the boys for the last month. He was sort of their coach, too, and he simply *had* to be there for the first real game.

In the end, going was simpler, and besides, she did *not* want to keep Charles away from Clint. If her son had ever been happier, Candace hadn't known about it. She saw fewer and fewer letters home and the absence of calls and letters from Eric no longer seemed to oppress him. So no. No way, no how, no chance, baby, would she let this thing with her and Clint come between Clint and Charles.

They sat in the Blackwell pew, she and Clint and Charles and the four boys, while Alice chose to sit up front with a trio of women about her age. During the service Clint stretched his arm along the back of the pew behind Charles, who sat between them. A couple of times his fingers brushed her shoulder, and she found herself growing angry over all of this.

When it came right down to it, Clint Blackwell had no right to complicate the situation the way he had. Sure, the feelings and interest and attraction between them had been there from the start, and sure, they had grown with time rather than diminished. And sure, her own reactions to him were just as strong as his apparently were to her, and she sometimes caught herself daydreaming about a future with him and all the rest. So, sure, it was mutual and growing stronger by the day. But that didn't mean they should do anything about it!

There was a child involved, and that changed the whole complexion of romantic relationships. With a child involved, you didn't—or shouldn't—have the freedom just to follow up on an interest and see where it took you. Eric had, and it had taken him away from his son. As a parent, Candace owed Charles more security in his future than he'd had in his past. She owed him the knowledge that she wouldn't bring someone into his life, make him too important—too *paren-tal*—when there was a huge chance that things wouldn't work out. What was the divorce rate these days, anyway? One out of two? Assuming it would ever even get that far.

No. She would not take chances with her child's security for the sake of some...dalliance. And what was the matter with Clint that he didn't see the potential dangers, too? He was supposed to be something of an expert with children, yet...

The service was over. They all stood for Josh Randall's closing prayer, and then Clint was moving into the aisle, pausing to let her and Charles out, too. The older boys were apparently on their own. With Charles ahead of her, and Clint too close behind, she followed the crowd out of the church, conscious of Clint's hand, proprietary and warm as it rested on her back, her shoulder, her elbow, her waist.

"Let's go change," Clint said, when they were outside and standing in soft spring sunshine. "I'll get the picnic basket and meet you guys out back by the diamond."

"Okay," Candace said, then caught her lower lip between her teeth as she watched him walk away.

He had a certain...energy in his step that she didn't remember being there when they first met. A certain...*life* in his eyes that seemed somehow new.

It struck her for the first time that maybe she and Charles had filled a gap in Clint's life the same way he had filled the holes in theirs.

And if so, maybe . . .

No.

She sighed and watched him, broad shouldered and lean, until he rounded a corner and was out of her sight.

He was something, that was for sure.

"Mom?"

She looked down to find Charles frowning up at her. "What, sweetie?"

"We're supposed to be going to get our clothes and change."

They had lunch on a blanket in the fresh-mown back field. A dozen or so other families were doing the same, while some people went home to eat and then came back, and some left for good, having no interest in coming to watch the game.

During lunch they talked baseball and strategy and good sportsmanship, with Bobby, Ray, Ian and Dean antsy and keyed up. Clint himself was relaxed and happy and couldn't remember feeling this good in a long, long time. He lounged on his side, propped up on an elbow, listening to the boys plot and letting his gaze and thoughts roam to Candace every couple of minutes or so.

Just her being there made the day feel complete. She was quieter than usual this day, a little sober and subdued, but after his antics Friday night and his declarations yesterday, her continued presence in his life told Clint a lot. He hadn't scared her off, and he'd been worried about that. Fresh out of a divorce, he'd known she probably wouldn't jump at any entanglements. And she hadn't. Still, she hadn't bolted, either, and that told him they had a chance.

He wouldn't push. He was a man of some patience. So as long as she didn't withdraw from him, he'd consider they were moving ahead.

"Hey, Clint," Ian said, jumping up and brushing crumbs off his jeans, "let's hit the field. We want to be good and warmed up by the game."

The rest of the boys, Charles included, got to their feet. Clint, lazy, content, and loath to move, waved them off. "You guys go ahead. You don't need me. I think I'll just lie here and relax a few minutes."

The older boys accepted this and trotted off to get the equipment and take it to the ball diamond. Charles stood, frowning.

"C'mon, Clint. We need you to tell us what to do."

"I'll be over in a couple of minutes, Charlie," Clint said. "Go ahead and help the boys get set up."

Charles opened his mouth to argue, then sent a frown Candace's way. "Why don't you come over, Mom? You can help in the outfield or something."

"Charles, I haven't played softball in twenty years," Candace said. "I really don't think I'd be much help. Go on, though. Your team is waiting for you."

He started to protest again, then clamped his jaw shut and jammed his Stetson on his head. "All right," he said, and stalked off, back stiff, shoulders high, mouth set.

"What's wrong with him?" Clint asked, frowning after him.

"I have no idea," Candace said. But in the back of her mind another incident rose to connect with this one, and she began to think that maybe she knew.

"Strike one!" the umpire called, and Ray, pitching to Peter Drake, grinned.

The last time they'd played Drake's team, the principal had gotten three runs off Ray's pitches. Today Ray was ignoring the chip on his shoulder and paying attention to Clint's signals, and everything was going a whole lot better.

It was the bottom of the sixth. Drake's team had a man on third itching to come home.

"Strike two!" the ump called, and curly-haired Ray nearly split his face grinning.

Clint, playing catcher, licked his lips. The pitch had been good, and worked, but it had *not* been what he'd called. Just like the last time. He'd signaled a fastball, and Ray had thrown a curve.

"Time!" Clint called, holding up two fingers and trotting out to Ray on the mound. He flipped up the catcher's mask and leaned close to Congregational's young pitcher.

"Okay, Ray, you're doing great. You've gotten two past him and we only need one more to close the inning." Also, the teams were tied pointwise and that meant they'd have a good chance now to get ahead. "Now, listen. I don't know what you're thinking out here, but this isn't grudge time, it's a ball game. That last pitch was not what I called.''

"I know," Ray said, frowning. "But I just thought the curve would be good for one more—"

"He only missed it by an eighth of an inch. He's a fast learner, Ray. Remember that. If you throw one more curve ball, he's not going to miss it. Let's go with a fast ball this time, just a little bit to the inside edge of the plate. Okay?''

Ray licked his lips, nodded. "Okay, Coach. Fast ball to the inside.''

Clint flipped the mask back down and trotted back to crouch behind home plate.

Pete Drake, hatless and wearing old gray sweat pants and a T-shirt, grinned at him over his shoulder, then turned his gaze back to the pitcher. "Forget the strategy, Blackwell," he said, ready to swing. "I've got it this time. This baby's going all the way past the Johnny-on-the-spot.''

On the mound Ray was winding up. *Fast ball*, Clint thought. *Inside*.

"In your dreams, Drake," Clint said, eyes on Ray. "You just watch and . . .''

Ray threw the ball, fast and hard. And inside.

And high. Peter Drake jumped back, but not fast enough.

A sickening thunk sounded as the ball connected with his face, and then he fell backward, and Clint saw the blood.

* * *

"Your nose!" Frieda Dale cried, having pushed through the group surrounding Drake to kneel at his side. "Oh, Pete, you broke your beautiful nose!"

Peter Drake tried to shake his head to clear it, then groaned with the effort. On his back in the dirt, he squinted his eyes open. "Frieda," he said. "I didn't know you were here."

His movements had started the blood flowing again, and Clint moved in to press another white handkerchief to Peter Drake's nose.

Frieda winced, but kept her place at his side and didn't let go of the principal's hand.

"It is broken, isn't it, Clint?" she said, tears in her dark eyes.

"Definitely," Clint said, then glanced at the woman. "He's lucky he didn't break his beautiful head. Or take the hit in one of his beautiful eyes."

Frieda flushed at this, realizing how much she had revealed upon rushing up to Drake.

"He needs to get to the hospital," Clint said. "Shall I take him or—"

"No," Frieda said. "Help me get him to the car. I'll take him."

Holding the blood-sodden handkerchief to his nose, Peter Drake managed to get to his feet; mostly on his own, now that the initial dazedness had worn off.

Frieda pulled his left arm around her shoulders and held him around the waist, encouraging the big lanky man to lean on her petite frame.

"I think we can manage," Frieda said to Clint. And Drake, Clint noticed, seemed to think they could manage just fine, despite the blood and mess and pain.

The crowd watched the pair until Frieda had helped him into her little Toyota. Then Clint blew out a breath and turned to look at the rest of the players and fans.

"Well, gang, what'll it be? You want to play this one out or what?"

But the enthusiasm for the game had gone. Peter Drake could have had a lot more than a broken nose from a solid hit like that. They'd been talking about making protective headgear a rule rather than an option, but somehow, they'd never gotten around to actually cementing the thought. Now, Clint thought, it was time.

"Let's call it a tie," someone suggested, and murmurs of agreement swept through the small crowd.

"Okay," Clint said. "Come on, boys, let's get the equipment together and wrap things up."

People drifted off, picking up bats and balls and any trash left around the small set of bleachers. As Clint went back to where they'd left the blanket and picnic basket, he caught sight of Ray, nearly hidden by the fat trunk of an oak tree.

"Hey, Ray," Clint said, wandering over, using a baseball bat like a walking stick.

Startled, the boy scrubbed at his face, straightened his shoulders, lifted his chin.

"Hey, Clint," he said, looking off to where the trees grew thicker in the acres behind the church.

"We're going to call the game a tie," Clint said.

Ray nodded.

Clint waited, but the boy didn't seem to want to talk. Sensing he needed to be alone a while longer, Clint turned to head back to their picnic site.

"Clint?"

He stopped, turned. "Yeah?"

"I didn't do that on purpose. I never tried to hit him."

His voice cracked a bit on this and Clint looked away, then back. "I know," he said. "Accidents happen."

"Clint?"

"Yeah?"

"When you see Mr. Drake—you know, after he gets out of the hospital?"

"Yeah, Ray?"

"Would you tell him it was an accident?"

"I'm sure he knows that, Ray." Because no matter how tough and nasty the boys liked to act, anyone who knew them, especially Ray, knew they weren't vicious. Trying to pound the principal in a game was one thing. Trying to hurt him physically was something else. And even if Ray had doubts about himself, Clint didn't. And, he was sure, neither did Peter Drake.

"Still," Ray said, "I'd like him to hear it. And...tell him I'm really sorry."

"I'm sure he knows that, too, Ray," Clint said. "But I have a feeling *you're* not going to know that until you go see him and tell him yourself."

"Jeez, that was awful," Charles said, helping Candace pick up the few stray napkins and bits of trash that had been blown away from picnic sites by the breeze.

"Yes," Candace said. "It was. I'm just glad he's going to be okay. It could have been a lot more serious."

Charles, still wide-eyed over the whole experience, shook his head. "I don't think I've ever seen so much blood! And the way he just lay there at first—I thought he was dead!"

Candace shivered just thinking about it. There had been a horrible moment when she'd thought the same thing.

And it could have happened; just that fast, anything could have happened. One minute the man had been there, grinning and wisecracking. And the next he'd been sprawled in the dirt, blood spurting, nothing else moving. It could have been worse. And it could have been Clint.

Or there could be a car accident on the way home.

Or his horse could spook and throw him or any freak thing.

Mortality.

Sitting in the bleachers, she'd seen Frieda Dale hurtle herself out of the crowd and over to Drake's side.

She'd seen the terror—and the love—on the woman's face and had needed to know no more.

And the way her guts had wrenched at the thought that it could have been Clint had told her plenty about herself, too.

She loved the man. It had become too, too clear in those few seconds.

"Boy," Charles said, dropping a paper plate into their trash bag, "did you see Mrs. Dale fly out there? I bet things are going to start changing for those two from now on."

"I wouldn't doubt it," Candace said, picking up a piece of waxed paper. "Sometimes things like that make you realize things you didn't know you knew."

"Well, I don't see how they didn't know," Charles said. "Everybody else has known for a long time." Then he frowned, his movements slowing, and he cast her a glance that snagged her full attention.

"What's wrong, Charles?"

He shrugged. "You know, everybody knew that Mr. Drake and Mrs. Dale liked each other, because of the way they looked at each other all the time."

"Mmm-hmm," Candace said.

"And everybody...everybody knows it about you and Clint, too."

Candace's jaw dropped. "Charles, I don't—"

He shook his head, determined now to speak on the subject. "Everybody can tell," he insisted. "The guys at the ranch talk about it all the time."

Candace put a hand to her forehead. "Charles..."

"But the thing is," Charles went on, looking terribly small and hurt and vulnerable. "The thing I keep wondering about lately is this. Mom, do you think Clint's only been nice to me so you'd like him better?"

Oh, God, Candace thought and felt all the good things that had happened for her son start to crash down around them.

"Hey, you two," Clint said, coming up to them, picnic basket in one hand. Candace remembered the first time they'd seen him, Clint strolling up his driveway, messy from an egg fight with the boys, the empty egg basket swinging from his fingers.

It seemed like so long ago.

Then he had been a client, a stranger.

Today he was such an important part of their lives.

A part so important that his absence would leave a deep hole.

Mom, do you think Clint's only been nice to me so you'd like him better?

"What's going on?" Clint said, picking up on the somberness that resulted from Candace and Charles's conversation.

"Nothing," Candace said, forcing a smile.

She'd known that to let herself get involved with him—with anyone—would be a huge mistake. Now, even though she'd kept that involvement, on the outside at least, to a minimum, Charles was already paying for it. He'd found out he couldn't trust his father to consider him important in his life. Now he doubted Clint's motives, too. Somehow she had to find a way to reassure Charles that his relationship with Clint wasn't phony. And that his caring for the boy had nothing to do with her.

"You doing okay, Charlie?" Clint said, studying him.

"Sure," Charles said, but didn't follow up with the usual "Clinty."

Clint gave Candace a questioning look.

She shrugged a little, unable to explain.

"Well," Clint said, trying to change the mood, "since the game was called and we have the rest of the afternoon free, I had an idea. Why don't we pick up a bunch of hot dogs and hamburgers and go back to the ranch and have a big old Sunday barbecue? We can invite the boys—maybe cheer Ray up—and Alice could invite a couple of her friends."

Normally an idea like this would have had Charles begging—or at least insisting. Today, now that his thoughts had been voiced, they clung to him, weighed him down.

"That sounds like fun, Charles," Candace said, desperate to restore the old relationship between Charles and Clint. "I think we should do it."

He looked at her and she realized her enthusiasm had been a mistake. Suspicion lurked in that glance. Suspicion that said of course she'd want to go and of course Clint would ask them. They were as loony for each other as Mrs. Dale and Mr. Drake.

"Oh, wait," Candace said, snapping her fingers and looking dismayed. "I forgot. I've got a case to work on for tomorrow. I promised Jack I'd have a bunch of stuff all ready for him."

She saw Clint's disappointment and Charles's twinge of surprise.

"We could make it quick," Clint said. "You'd be home by early evening. You wouldn't be much longer than the ball game would have run—"

"No," Candace said. "I'd really better not. But Charles, if you want to, you can go. There's no reason for you to miss out on anything just because I have to work. Don't you think so, Clint? I mean, if you're still going to do something out at the Double C."

For one instant she saw that he wasn't. That the proposed barbecue had been mentioned with her in mind. That they'd make it a party, but they'd make it a party as a couple, host and hostess. If it hadn't made for such a horrible complication, she knew the realization would have thrilled her. As it was, it weighed on her. As did Clint's reaction to her suggestion to take Charles.

Oh, please, she thought. *Please know the right thing to do.*

"Sounds good to me," Clint said, barely missing a beat. "How about it, Charles? Just because your mom wants to be an old stick-in-the-mud doesn't mean we should waste our day of rest, does it?"

Charles's chin jerked up, eyes hopeful as he raised them to the tall rancher. "No," he said carefully, studying Clint for the truth. "I guess not."

"*Guess* not?" Clint said. "Of *course* not! Come on, Charlie, let's go invite the guys."

Then they moved off, Charles picking up spark and life as they went. By the time they'd crossed the field to where Ian and Dean were collecting equipment, Charles was walking like his old self—his *new* old self. The self that had emerged under the care and tutelage of Clint Blackwell. The self that was still fragile and insecure and could be broken by anything Charles might see as a breach of trust or a hint of rejection.

Oh, boy, Candace thought, letting out a long breath. Clint had salvaged this moment of insecurity, but what would happen with the next?

And *how* was she supposed to do this thing that she needed to do? Just how was she going to keep their relationship good and her own with Clint...non-existent?

Because it already existed and grew every day. She loved him, and that did not make her happy. Aside from any potential parting of the ways, there was now a new problem. If she didn't stay away from Clint, Charles would always wonder where Clint's true motives lay.

Oh, boy. she thought again. *Oh, boy, oh, boy, oh, boy.*

"So what's wrong with you and your mom to-day?" Clint asked Charles as they drove the pickup over to the IGA for barbecue supplies, Clint and Charles in the cab, the older boys clowning around in the back.

"I don't know," Charles said. "Nothing, I guess. Hey, can we get chips and dip, too?"

"Sure," Clint said, turning the truck one-handedly into the grocery store drive. "We can get anything we want. Hey, Charlie? Tell me something. Do you think your mom just didn't want to come out tonight? I mean, I know she has work to do, but I wondered if maybe she was upset about something or didn't feel well or..."

Charles shrugged, then looked out his side window. "I don't know, Clinty. She didn't exactly tell me, but I think she wanted to get home for something else."

"Yeah?" Clint said. "What?"

"Well—" Charles sighed and kept looking out the window "—I guess I shouldn't say anything, so don't tell her I did. But I'm pretty sure she wanted to get home early today because I think she has a date."

"A...*date?*" Clint said.

"A date, you know," Charles said, then grinned. "Hey, can we get some Twinkies, too? For dessert, I mean. And some—"

"Sure," Clint said blankly. "Sure."

A date?

He turned off the engine and just sat for a second, staring, while Charles, grinning, bounced out of the cab and the boys vaulted out of the back.

Chapter Nine

After that day at the ball game, Candace began a new way of dealing with Clint. It seemed not only right but imperative to keep treating him in the same fashion. What she had struggled to find a solution for since the beginning—a way to uninvolve herself with Clint Blackwell—had taken care of itself from the ball game on.

"I'd like to go out and ride Coyote tonight after school," Charles said that next Monday. "But you don't have to stay if you don't want. I mean, if you could just drop me off... I know you have work and things to do."

The following Sunday, while Charles didn't exactly try to persuade her not to go to church with him, he did corner Clint after service and then came back to tell her he wanted to spend the day at the ranch—and that Clint had said he could ride out with him, so unless she really wanted to go, he'd go without her and call when he was done.

Candace smiled through all of this, acted like his so thoughtful arrangements simplified her life enormously, but inside, of course, she felt rejected, abandoned, lonely and hurt. While she understood Charles's quest for reassurance about Clint's caring for *him*, she was getting, after two weeks of this, to the point of needing a little reassurance of somebody's caring for *her*. The two people she cared most about in the world were together while she spent virtually all of her free time home alone.

She also found it strange that Clint hadn't called or come in during the times he'd dropped Charles off. When she saw him at church, or briefly at the ranch, he was pleasant but distant, holding himself aloof. Of course, if Charles made him feel as welcome in his relationship with Candace as he made Candace feel in his relationship with Clint, everything else made perfect sense. Charles wanted the two of them apart and made no bones about it.

And while Candace knew she should be glad—it really did simplify things enormously—she wasn't glad. Mostly she alternated between feeling like a noble martyr and feeling like a big and stupid fool.

School was out.

The days grew downright hot, and Candace had shifted her office things to work at home. Charles had made it through the second grade without Peter Drake having to expel him.

"The boy's made an amazing turnaround," Drake had said the week after Bobby's pitch had broken his nose. Candace had gone to school one evening for the final parent-teacher conference of the year, an evening when Charles was having dinner at the Double C with Clint and Alice and she was going home again to Lean Cuisine and frozen corn on the cob. Drake's cheekbones and eyes were still purple, the nose still bandaged, big and white. But he seemed happy and relaxed and laughed a lot. And Frieda Dale, who smiled a lot herself, was sporting a new diamond solitaire. Not flashy or huge, but enough to spark Candace out of self-pity and into downright witchiness.

Well, isn't that special, she thought, looking at the ring, then catching herself. Jeez, jealousy could make you a lousy person.

"Congratulations," she told Frieda and managed to mean it. Frieda and Peter Drake were good people and deserved each other. Deserved happiness.

As did Charles.

And when Candace remembered to focus on the fact that she really was doing the right and selfless thing for her child, the rest didn't hurt so much.

Or even if it did, on those nights when the two people she wanted most to be with were off together without her, it was some consolation to know with some certainty that she was, at last, doing what she'd come to Cedar Grove to do.

After fourteen years she had finally put her priorities in order.

And as a mother, it felt good to finally know that as far as her son was concerned, she was, at last, doing the right thing.

"Okay, everybody," Clint Blackwell said, holding up his hands to get the boys' attention, "we've got a lot of work to get done today. It's supposed to rain this afternoon and that whole chunk of fence on the south boundary is down. Ian, I want you to. . ."

A bronze BMW swept up the drive, and Clint lost his thought, his gaze focusing on the car.

Candace had barely stopped the car when Charles, as usual, hopped out, waving to him with his Stetson. It was June now, and hot. Clint had told Charles they needed to get him a straw hat for summer, but Charles said he liked the tan felt one just fine.

As Charles rounded the front of the car and headed toward them, Candace, as usual, began to back up and turn the car around.

Let her go, his mind told him, and his mouth firmed into a hard line.

She doesn't want to be here, she doesn't want to see you, just let her go.

His mind had been telling him that for weeks now, though, and letting her go wasn't making anything one bit better.

"Ian," he said, "you're in charge. Get the equipment together and go mend fence."

Without taking his eyes off Candace, he left the boys behind, nodded to the approaching Charles and headed for the BMW.

"Hey!" he called, swinging his hat over his head to get her attention. "Hey, Candace! Wait a minute!"

She saw him, and he saw her hesitate. He broke into a trot and, from behind him, heard Charles. "Hey, Clint! Mom's in a hurry—"

"Too bad," Clint tossed over his shoulder. "I don't think this can wait."

He looked good.

To Candace, after all these weeks of barely seeing him, Clint Blackwell running toward her looked so darned *good.*

Her chest tightened and her throat ached. She shoved the gearshift into park, waiting, but didn't turn off the car. She wasn't staying. She'd seen Charles's mutinous look as Clint passed him and headed for her.

Mom? Do you think Clint's only been nice to me so you'd like him better?

Mrs. Dale and Mr. Drake look at each other the same way you and Clint do. Everybody knows it. The boys talk about it all the time.

"Hi," Clint said, stopping about five feet away from the car, breathing deeply from the run, chest rising and falling under his red T-shirt.

"Hi," Candace said. *Long time no see.* If absence was a test of real feeling, she'd either passed the test stunningly—or failed miserably, depending on your point of view.

Why couldn't seeing him now have been no big deal, a bland yet friendly meeting that made her wonder what all the tumult had been about in times past? Why did those gray eyes, that windblown hair, that half smile, have to make her feel so good—and so bad?

"Got a minute?" he asked.

"I..."

She looked away for an instant, thinking, weighing. And saw Charles standing halfway between Clint and the boys over by the barn, hands on hips, little mouth set, watching and waiting to see what she and Clint were going to do.

"I..." she said again, feeling pulled ten thousand different ways.

"Look," Clint said, not smiling anymore, "I know you're in a hurry. I've got things to do, too. But..."

"But?"

"I really think we should talk."

"Talk," Candace said, glancing again at her son. *Do you think Clint's only been nice to me so you'd like him better?*

No.

No matter how tempting spending a few minutes or days or months or years with Clint Blackwell was, she couldn't do this to Charles. Especially after Eric's rejection and betrayal. She did not have the right to follow her own heart at the risk of breaking her son's.

"What did you need to talk about?" she asked, and made a show of glancing at her watch.

"Come inside," he said. "We'll have coffee. And... talk."

"Is it about Charles? I mean, is anything wrong? Is he doing all right?"

"Charles is fine," Clint said, and she began to see him withdrawing from her, his eyes, warm one second, cooling, hardening gray now.

This was the first attempt he'd made to restore things between them in weeks.

Now...

Now, Candace knew, the mood and moment for that had passed. A part of her shriveled at the knowledge. But the larger part of her knew she had done the right thing.

"Never mind," Clint said, then nodded. "I'd better get to work."

"Okay," Candace said, fingers curling around the leather-covered steering wheel.

Then, as she sat there, Clint turned and walked away.

Beyond him stood Charles.

Candace knew she should have felt gratified by the boy's obvious relief at Clint's return. Charles relaxed visibly, said something to Clint, then cheerily waved goodbye to her.

Clint put a hand on Charles's shoulder, and together they went to join the group of Clint's boys.

Candace, biting her lower lip until it hurt, put the car in reverse and drove away.

The summer crawled on, each day becoming hotter and longer, and work on the ranch now continued until dark; and dark came after eight p.m. Since Candace couldn't think of any excuse except the selfish desire for her son's company to refuse his daily requests to go to the Double C, Candace had too much time on her hands.

At least back home that had never been a problem. Too much time? What an odd concept. But here, now, she was beginning to feel that time was about all she had.

"Morgan?" she said into the phone. "Hi, it's Candace." And, she realized, it was "Candace" for the third time that week. If she didn't get a life soon, her long-distance bills to LA were going to be hideous.

"Okay, let's have it," Morgan Larkenshire said, with typical Morgan straightforwardness. "Enough is enough, Candace. You ready to talk about it or do you just want me to hop on a plane and come help you move back?"

Dear Dad,

Thanks for the new software you sent. I haven't tried it out, because I've been really busy out at the Double C and I haven't had a chance. Me and

Clint and the guys work from morning till dark, but it's not really like work. Mostly we have a great time.

Anyway, the word-processing program looks great and so does the rest of the stuff. I'm going to try it out as soon as I get the chance.

Only thing is, I think things are going to get even busier. Clint's taking me to a horse show this weekend. There's this club around here called 4-H and it's their horse show and Clint thinks I might want to join. I'm not sure about it, but Clint says he did it when he was a kid and it was great. He showed me the trophies and ribbons he won and says I've learned to ride well enough I could win some, too. I'll probably join and try it out because Clint says that's the only way you find out if something is good, and Clint usually knows.

Anyway, thanks again for the computer stuff and I'll write when I can.

If you're interested, I'll let you know how the 4-H thing turns out, even though I know you're not into animals and stuff.

Sincerely,
Charles

"A horse show?" Candace said, talking to Clint from inside her car. She'd brought Charles this morning as she had every morning. And she'd always stayed right in the car, pretending to be too busy to stay.

Mostly, after that last time, Clint ignored her. Once in a while Alice came out and they chatted for a few minutes, and Candace realized how much she missed Alice's company, too.

They'd become like family for a few months. Candace wanted to know about the little things, the pie baking, goings-on at the church, whether she'd gotten the oven thermostat fixed since they'd last baked together and charcoaled two blueberry pies.

Blueberry. Clint's favorite.

Now Charles's favorite, too.

"Yeah, a horse show," Clint said, standing outside the car. "Tomorrow. It starts around noon, but I'd like to get there around eleven."

"It sounds like fun," Candace said, thinking that that was a huge understatement. Right this second she thought she wanted to go to that horse show with Clint and Charles and Alice more than she'd ever wanted to go anywhere in her whole life.

"You wouldn't like it, Mom," Charles said.

Candace lowered her eyes, not wanting anyone to see how much that stung.

"I think she'd like it fine," Clint said, aware of the undercurrents suddenly running between mother and son. "Unless, of course, you have other plans, Candace. Business? Errands? A date, maybe?"

Candace's mouth curved in a wry smile. "No," she said. "No date. I suppose, though, that I should try to catch up on some work at home."

"Probably," Charles chimed in. "I know how you're always talking about getting a chance to scrape the windows—"

"Scrape the windows?" Clint said, looking from one to the other of the Whitney duo. He'd noticed a tension between them for weeks but had put it down to Charles's probable reaction to his mother starting to date again. Yet . . . Candace had wanted to come to the horse show. She had been going to say yes, he could see it in her eyes.

And then Charles had piped up, making excuses for her. And her eyes, jade green and sparkling, had gone flat, dead, just that quickly.

"Charles," Clint said, without looking away from Candace, "go help Ian get the horses saddled up."

"But—"

"Please," Clint said firmly. "Go help Ian. I need to talk to your mother."

"No," Charles said, and Clint glanced at him, hearing the note of alarm in his voice.

The boy's eyes were wide, his breathing quick, his gaze darting anxiously from Clint to his mother.

"Yes," Clint said and took the step forward to open Candace's car door. He bent, took her elbow, helped her out.

"Clint, I probably should be going. . . ."

Clint slammed the door.

"What you probably should be doing is telling me what is going on here. Whatever it is, I think it's gone on long enough. Don't you?"

Still holding her elbow, he flashed an impatient look at Charles.

"I said go help Ian," Clint said, sounding every inch the boss. "I meant it. Now move out."

Charles started to argue, then fury and outrage hardened his face. "You got it," he said and turned and ran toward the barn.

Candace, knowing that his rage came from pain, wanted to go after him.

"Wait," Clint said, restraining her. "Ian's there. He'll be okay. Level with me, Candace. Please. What's going on?"

Ten minutes later he was staring at her, eyes narrowed, an expression of disbelief and something too near scorn marring his features.

"Let me be sure I've got this straight," he said, standing in the living room while Candace sat on the edge of the couch, back straight, one ear cocked toward the outside, where Charles was off by himself no doubt feeling neglected and betrayed. "You're not going to the horse show because *Charles* doesn't want you to go?"

Clint didn't understand. Clint hadn't had to sit helplessly and watch a six-year-old shrivel with the growing knowledge that his distant father didn't particularly miss him after the move, that he rarely even had time to drop a note or pick up the phone. But he certainly had time for Gina and trips to Vail. Just like Clint had time for Candace.

Do you think he's only been nice to me so you'd like him better?

Lord. Clint hadn't had to hear that question, either.

"He feels *threatened,* Clint," Candace said, rising in frustration. "That little boy out there is just starting to heal. I owe most of that to you, I know. But I have to tell you that I'm not going to let me or you or anybody else hurt him like that again. So if that means I don't go to the horse show, I'm not going to the horse show."

"This isn't about a horse show," he said. "This is about letting a six-year-old run your life."

"I'm his mother. I'm putting him first. After all my mistakes have cost him in the past, I owe him that."

"You're giving him total control." He moved a step closer. "You're allowing him to lie and con and manipulate. You're making him into a tyrant."

"I'm going to talk to him about lying to you about my dating," she said. "But as for the rest, I'm just trying to stay clear of here so I can give him the security of knowing you care about him for *him,* and not for me. I think his lying to you shows just how desperate and scared he feels."

"He knows I care about him," Clint said. "And if he doesn't yet, he will in time. It'll come on its own.

It's the only way it *can* come. With experience and time."

"Then maybe in time I'll—"

"No." Clint shook his head. "You're not getting it. If you continue to let him run things, all he's doing is creating a safe, no-risk situation. Staying in that isn't going to reassure him of anything."

"What do you mean?"

"Let's take a marriage, for example. Let's take a jealous husband who won't allow his wife out of the house because he's afraid she'll find somebody else."

"What does that have to do with—"

"Just hear me out. The only way that husband is going to find out if the wife *wants* anybody else is to let her go and see if she comes back. The more she comes back, the more assured he gets. I mean, where is the assurance if the relationship in question is never put to the test?"

Candace turned away from him, crossed her arms, wandered over toward the cold stone fireplace. "Maybe you're right."

"I know I'm right. Believe me, Candace, you're not doing that kid any favors by letting him call all the shots. What's going to happen when he gets a little older and goes out into the big mean world and finds out it doesn't really revolve around him after all? You owe it to him to prepare him for that. A child needs rules, boundaries. A six-year-old child is *not* equipped to make the decisions in this life. You're the parent, Candace. You're not here to make him happy or to make him your friend. You have a job to do, plain and simple. A hard job. But if you don't do it, he's headed for big trouble.''

Candace raked her nails through her hair. "I also owe it to him to protect him wherever I can. I don't know. Sometimes it's so hard to know what's right.''

"I know," Clint said.

She turned away from the fireplace and found he'd come closer. The only light in the big living room came from the windows. He stood in soft shadow, only a few feet away. Her fingers curled into fists to keep her from going to him.

"What I do know," she said, trying to summon up a detached, courtroom voice, "is that he's out there right now feeling betrayed. Feeling that you're in here because you'd rather spend the time with his mother than with him.''

"Sometimes I would," Clint said. "I don't see anything wrong with that. Any more than I'd resent it if he wanted to spend the day playing with his friends.''

"This is different," Candace said.

"Not really.''

But it was, and they could stand here talking about it all day and he still wouldn't get it. She felt disappointed in his lack of grasp of the situation—and disappointed, too, that Charles didn't seem to be Clint's first concern. She remembered that first meeting when she'd sensed some interest in him, that little spark of something you feel when the chemistry clicks.

Yes, she'd felt that spark, too, and it had grown and deepened and all the rest. And yes, it would be nice if she didn't have to think about anything else but following her feelings and falling into his arms.

But she was an adult now. An adult with a vulnerable child.

She had to think about that first, and it bothered her to realize that Clint might not have that same kind of commitment.

Do you think he's only been nice to me so you'd like him better?

No, she'd never thought that.

Now, though, now that she'd leveled with him and seen his response, a seed of doubt had been planted. And maybe it wasn't fair to Clint and maybe she was just too sensitive on the issue, wary and looking for potential trouble and finding it anywhere she could.

Maybe that was all there was to it.

Or maybe not.

Either way, though, the seed, insidious and ugly, was now there.

"I have to go talk to Charles," Candace said.

He only nodded, watching her in the morning shadows.

She'd nearly reached the door before he spoke.

"While you're at it, tell him something he might as well know."

Candace turned, hand on the doorknob.

Clint turned to look at her. "Tell him I love you. Tell him I love him, too. And tell him that if you two feel the same way about me, that's all we need. We can work this thing through.''

Candace couldn't respond.

Her throat closed and dried up. And she didn't know what she could say back to him, anyway.

Things were so complicated right now she couldn't even think.

One minute she doubted and resented him. The next she wanted nothing more than to go to him and . . .

And her son was out there in the barn, hurting.

She blinked back the sudden tears in her eyes and nodded, then slipped out the door.

I love you, too, Clint, she thought.

But it wasn't that simple.

And giving in to the urge to tell him how she felt about him wouldn't solve anything.

She closed the door behind her, dried her eyes and went to find her son.

Chapter Ten

Clint felt like the good, the bad and the ugly.

Good, because he'd finally come out with his feelings for Candace and Charles. Bad, because she'd felt no such compulsion to say how she felt about him.

And ugly, because he'd hit her with some hard truths about what she was doing to that kid.

Not that he didn't understand her point and her motives. Both were good. He just didn't believe her projected outcome was accurate.

And it was frustrating to know that he had no right to do anything about it.

Charles didn't belong to him.

Candace didn't belong to him.

He wandered into the kitchen, and the daytime dimness and silence of the unlit, empty house taunted him.

Alice was shopping in town, Charles was probably crying in the barn, Candace was trying to console him, and Clint... Clint had no rightful place in anything that was going on out there.

He stopped at the kitchen window over the sink and stared at the barn. The refrigerator hummed, and Alice's cat clock ticked, and out in the barn his whole life went on without him.

He dropped his head back, rolled it from side to side, feeling the knots in his neck and hearing them snap, crackle and pop.

"Clint!"

The yell, muffled by the house, came from outside.

Clint's head snapped up and he saw Candace running from the barn.

"Clint! Charles! Clint!"

He rushed for the door and met her on the porch, halfway, catching her by the elbows.

"What? What is it, Candace? What's wrong?"

"It's Charles!" she said, gasping and crying. "Charles is *gone!*"

"He said you *told* him to," Ian said, frantic to explain. "He said you told him to get Coyote and go down to Doc Long's and pick up some syringes for the distemper shots."

"What?" Clint stared. "We did the distemper shots last week! Where did he get that idea?"

"He's run away," Candace said flatly, holding herself with crossed arms. "He's taken the horse and run away."

"Don't jump to conclusions," Clint said, looking around, looking for... what? Clues?

Lord.

"Did you see him ride out?" he asked Ian.

"Not really. I was trying to—"

"So you don't know which direction he actually went."

"No, not really."

"Any of you guys see him?"

Bobby, Dean and Ray shook their heads.

"Okay," Clint said. "You guys saddle up and head out. Cover the ranch. Split up and check back here every couple of hours."

"But he told Ian he was going to the vet's house," Candace said. "Isn't that about a half mile that way?" She pointed toward the highway that led to town.

"Right," Clint said. "That's where you and I are going. I'm assuming Charles told them that so he could get off the ranch without being stopped. But I'm sending the boys out to look on the Double C because Charles is just smart enough to have said that to throw us completely off.

"Let's go, everybody," he said, heading for the house, Candace running to keep up. "Do you want to stay here and see if he turns up, or do you want to come and help me look?''

"I want to go find him," Candace said, ill with images of a six-year-old out there alone. "Alice will be back soon, and I'll leave him a note. Besides, I don't think he's coming back. Not here."

Clint gave her a grim look and grabbed his keys off a hook. "Let's get moving, then. If we don't catch up with him right away, we'll start canvassing the neighbors."

"And call the police," Candace said, walking toward the kitchen phone. "That's what we'd better do first."

"We will," Clint said, opening the front door. "But it'll be quicker if we do it from the truck."

"You have a car phone?" Candace hurried to follow him outside.

"A CB. We'll get on the emergency channel and put the word out while we're looking."

They scrambled into the truck, and Clint had it started and moving before Candace had even shut her door.

They stopped at the home of Hank Long—a local vet and Clint's nearest neighbor—just in case.

"No," Hank said, emerging from a box stall where he'd been tending a wounded horse. "Nobody stopped here. But I did see a little blond kid riding a big bay on my way back from town a little bit ago."

"That's him," Candace said. "That's Charles. Where was he? How long ago? Did he look like he was okay?"

"On the outskirts of town," Hank said calmly. "I'd say it was probably thirty-five, forty minutes ago. He looked fine. If he hadn't, I probably would have noticed and thought to check it out."

"Thank God," Candace said, biting her lip. If she'd ever thought she'd known guilt and fear before, she'd been wrong.

"Let's go," Clint said, then thanked the doctor and swung himself back up into the cab of the truck.

They flew down the highway and stopped when they got to town.

There was no sign of Charles, of course, and as the choices of roads broadened and multiplied, they had no idea which way to go.

"If he's really running away," Candace said, "maybe he'd stop at home to get some of his stuff."

"Right," Clint said and headed for Cherry Lane.

The local police were scouring the county for a boy on a horse.

That was the first mistake, Clint and Candace realized after they stopped at the house. Precious minutes were wasted while Candace went through Charles's things, trying to figure out what was missing, looking for a clue to where he might go.

When you were six years old, Clint thought, trying to think like a kid, how large in scope could your plans

get? You ran away, took . . . what? Clothes. Money.
Peanut butter and jelly?

Then again, this was Charles.

"I don't see anything missing," Candace said. "But
he's been here. He changed clothes. And left these."

Clint looked up to see her holding Charles's previ-
ously favorite things. His boots, now scuffed and
broken in. His jeans, the knees and seat worn, nearly
the only thing he'd put on for weeks. And his hat. The
felt Stetson Clint hadn't been able to persuade him to
change for anything.

Clint closed his eyes.

And for the first time felt real fear crawl through his
belly.

"Clint?" Candace said, moments later. "Come
here. Come look at this."

She was standing at her kitchen window, looking
out over the backyard.

"Coyote," Clint said and rubbed his forehead hard.
The big bay was tied to the clothesline post, grass at his
feet, a dutch oven full of water close by.

"He didn't take the horse," Candace said, voice so
carefully controlled it sounded like a machine. "He
didn't take the horse or his boots or his jeans or his hat
and he's *not here!* This means something, Clint. *What
does it mean?*"

For one thing it meant the sheriff's search had been
wasted. They were looking for a kid on a horse and
Charles had obviously been off said horse for some
time.

For another thing it meant while they'd been searching the house Charles was that much farther ahead of them.

But how far?

Clint looked at his watch. Ten-fifteen. If Charles had left right after he'd been sent to the barn, he could have as much as an hour and a half on them by now.

God, Clint thought, *please let him be okay.*

Beeeep... "Candace? What's going on out there? And where the hell are you, anyway? I don't know what you've done to Charles, but this sure puts me in a hell of a mess! I'm picking him up at LAX tonight, so he'll be okay, but this isn't the end of it. God, how irresponsible can you be? That child *threatened me,* by the way! Threatened me...!"

Candace shut off the machine, snatched up the phone, punched in the numbers. "Eric," she said, "where is Charles now? What did he say? What's going on?"

He watched her talking to her ex-husband, seeing the relief mingle with new fears, new regrets, old guilts and failures and burdens.

He felt helpless and hapless, and while standing quietly he began to experience the weight of his own culpability here.

Go on, Charles. Now. Or whatever he'd said, playing the big tough authority figure.

He hadn't let Candace go after the boy, hadn't really placed much stock in her worries that Charles couldn't adjust to Clint having any relationship with Candace at all.

And now the boy was apparently making arrangements to fly to California.

His hands clenched into fists at his own insensitivity and stupidity.

Candace was not an idiot.

Candace knew her son.

And while he doubted that letting Charles run all over her like she had was the best thing, Clint also realized that his own methods had been even more wrong.

The kid had a real problem with trust, even after all this time. He should have known that, should have paid more attention. Should have, he realized, put the kid's needs over his own.

After being with Charles so much and so long, Clint really hadn't believed the old problems were still so strong.

But now...

He believed.

He didn't know what could be done to change it, but he definitely believed.

Candace hung up, promising Eric she would keep him informed. She ran through the other messages on the machine quickly, checking to see if any were from Charles, but they weren't. A couple were from Jack Harden at work, one was from her dentist, and most were from her ex-husband, growing angrier and more frantic every time he called.

Turning away from the machine, Candace took a deep breath and let it out.

"Charles is on his way to California," she said. "He made the ten o'clock commuter flight to Kansas City and he'll catch his connection to LA there. Eric says the next flight out of Cedar Grove is at noon. I've got to book a seat and pack."

"I'm coming with you," Clint said.

She looked at him, hesitated, then something changed in her eyes and he couldn't read them anymore. "No," she said. "Charles's father will be there and his stepmother. And me. I think everything is going to be complicated enough."

Clint swallowed, feeling his whole world slip through his fingers. "I'm sorry," he said. "This is all my fault."

"No," Candace said, opening the phone book to the yellow pages. "You were right. I've turned him into a tyrant. He called Eric and demanded he get him a flight and make the calls that would convince everyone to let a six-year-old travel alone. Told them it was an emergency and used his credit card to make it look completely legitimate."

She paused, marked a number in the phone book with an index finger, looked up at Clint with a weary flatness in her green eyes. "He had it all figured out, Clint. All Eric had to do was follow directions, or else."

"Or else what?"

"Or else he would really run away, of course. Just disappear and no one would ever see him again."

"Oh, boy," Clint said, rubbing his hand over his face.

"Yeah," Candace said and, finding the number for the little commuter airport that serviced Cedar Grove and surrounding communities, punched in the numbers and made her call.

The Grove County Airport was a little terminal with a couple of short runways built in the middle of what used to be Macon Grimes's clearest pasture.

Built and owned by Grimes's son Jared, it was the only airport around without having to drive to a city. The surrounding towns, Carter, Portia, Blakesville and Norton, combined with traffic from the larger Cedar Grove to give Jared Grimes a tidy little business. He routinely ran four flights to Kansas City a day, and three to St. Louis. From either of those cities, you could get anywhere in the world you wanted to go.

"Well, I guess this is it," Candace said, when Nita Shelley looked up from her desk and told the seven waiting passengers that it was time to board. The planes were twenty- to thirty-seaters. Nothing big and fancy, no in-flight food service, but always a cooler of cold Cokes and bags of salted nuts.

"I'll walk you out," Clint said, carrying her flight bag—all the luggage she'd packed. That had come as a huge relief to him—that she'd only packed enough for a day or two. He kept having this horrible sensation that once she set foot back in LA, he'd never see her again.

Her or Charles.

While Candace might not be planning anything like that now, he knew it could be arranged from there—movers hired, details handled by mail or phone. If they really wanted to, they could avoid coming to Cedar Grove ever again.

"Is there a number where I can reach you?" Clint asked, suddenly scared and needing this. "And how about an address?"

Candace frowned and joined the line of passengers standing on the tarmac. "I guess. But I'll be back in a day or two."

Maybe, Clint thought.

"Still," he said, trying to sound casual, "I'd like to be able to call. You know, find out how things went."

What I really want is to go with you! To solve this thing with Charles . . . and you . . . and bring my family home.

She dug in her handbag and pulled out a business card. "Eric's number," she said. "If you need me, he'll know where to reach me."

The line moved.

Candace moved with it.

Clint handed her the flight bag.

"Goodbye," he said. "Have a safe trip."

She nodded, managed a preoccupied smile and climbed the steps into the plane.

He stood there, waving like a fool until the plane disappeared.

Why did it feel like he might as well have said, "Goodbye. Have a good life."

Enough! Clint thought, still standing on the tarmac and getting a sudden image of himself and what he was doing—standing and gawking and mooning and internally whining to himself as he watched the plane's vapor trail disappear in the distance just like the plane. Just like his life.

What was he, anyway? A man or some wimped-out weenie?

Pulling himself together, he turned and walked toward the terminal. Candace didn't want him in California with her, and that was fine.

But *Clint* didn't want himself just standing around here doing nothing, while the rest of the parties involved—and possibly a couple of parties who weren't—settled this situation and decided his life. Weenies allowed that. Grown-up men took responsibility and actions to correct their past mistakes—and to determine their future.

"Hey, Nita," he said to the young blonde behind the counter, "I need your help. I need to check some flight schedules."

Five minutes later, he had what he wanted.

Then he sought and found Jared Grimes, owner and operator of Grove County Airport.

"I need to charter a plane," he said, then double-checked the schedule he'd copied. "How fast can you get me to Denver?"

With a quick connection in Kansas City, the ten a.m. flight that Charles took from Cedar Grove got into Denver thirty minutes before Clint's. The schedule said a two-hour layover. Clint hopped out of Jared Grimes's personal Cessna and told Jared to refuel, get something to eat and then wait.

He didn't know how long he'd be, but he knew the flight to LA would be boarding within the hour. He wasn't here to stop anybody from catching their plane. He was here to state his case, make amends and make things right.

Or at least, as right as they could be.

Maybe they couldn't be fixed at all, at least by him, but Clint wasn't buying into that. What had happened with Meg couldn't be fixed. He'd lost her and been helpless, and everything had been out of his control.

This was different.

He hoped.

At least with this he could try.

The airport was big, not as big as some he'd been to, but big enough. Inside, Clint checked his schedule again, noting airline and flight number. The gate was at the other end of the building, of course, and he found himself walking faster and faster, knowing he needed all the time he could get.

By the last leg of the trip, he was trotting. He slowed to a stop as he spotted a small blond head in the waiting room on his left.

Clint's heart thumped in his chest. Now that he was actually here, what was he going to do?

The boy, looking so small and vulnerable, gazed out the window, eyes blank and empty behind his coke-bottle glasses. As Clint watched, Charles poked the glasses up on his nose, and Clint, having seen that gesture so many times in so many situations, found that seeing it now wrenched at his guts.

He took a deep breath and approached him, but even when he got within three feet, Charles didn't turn to look.

"Hey, Pilgrim," Clint drawled, feeling sweat pop out on his upper lip, "I see you got an empty seat there next to you. Mind if I set a spell?"

Charles, obviously startled at first, recovered quickly. "It's a free country," he said. "Besides, if I don't like it, I can just move."

Oh, boy, Clint thought. Oh, boy, oh, boy, oh, boy.

Safely off the loud and bumpy little commuter plane out of Cedar Grove, Candace settled into the aisle seat of the 727 that would take her out of Kansas City. While the rest of the passengers boarded and the crew readied things for takeoff, Candace got her tickets out and rechecked the times. A forty-five minute layover in Denver. Not bad; hardly a layover at all. She'd have to check in half an hour before flight time, and by the time that was done, it would be practically time to board.

Then, on to LA.

On to her son.

On to... what?

What was going to happen when she went to take him home?

What was going to happen *if* she went to take him home?

If?

She bit her lip and wondered how long that thought had been growing in her mind.

But now that it was out, there was no pushing it back, back into the subconscious where the rest of the truths and fears and difficult knowledge liked to hide.

Yes, there was the possibility that they wouldn't be coming back.

Yes, there was the possibility that moving to Missouri had been a mistake all along.

You're regressing, Candace, that's all. Things haven't been easy here, so you're wanting to run home and lick your wounds. Listen, sweetheart...

Candace closed her eyes, shutting off the memory.

Maybe Eric had been right then.

Or maybe that's what she was considering doing now, too.

Clint.

Just the thought of him made her ache for him and all that she wanted to be.

Tell him I love you. Tell him I love him, too. And if you two feel the same about me, we can work this thing through.

Nice sentiment.

And maybe even true in some cases.

But in this case, Candace knew, it wasn't about love.

Yes, she believed Clint loved both her and her son.

Yes, she believed Charles loved Clint, and she did, too.

So everybody loves everybody, and that takes care of that.

But it didn't, not at all. Because love and trust had to go hand in hand. And both she and Charles had loved and trusted before and gotten burned—and Charles in fact had been scalded, left with scars forever.

If she'd begun to weaken on her stance, to think that if Charles would just give things a chance, they *could* all work things out together, this episode today had brought her right back to reality. Taking off to LA, even for Charles, was a radical move. And radical moves grew out of radical pain.

Because as much as he adored Clint and adored the Double C, Charles had been willing to give it all up rather than get more and more involved and get hurt again. A hard, horrible choice, but obviously the only one he could live with.

And the more she thought about it, Candace knew it was the only one she could feel safe and right about living with, too.

Chapter Eleven

"So where's Mom?" Charles said, staring straight ahead, feet swinging over the edge of the orange plastic contour chair.

"On her way to meet you in LA," Clint said.

Charles turned to look him full in the face for the first time. "You mean she's not with you? You're not together?" Frowning brows slanted over his wire-rimmed glasses.

"Nope. She didn't want me to go with her."

The frown deepened. "Why not?"

Clint shrugged. "What would it have accomplished? The reason you left was because you didn't want your mother and me to have a ten-minute conversation. How would us flying out together to get you make things any better?"

Charles, seeing the logic in this, shrugged and crossed his arms. The loafer-clad feet started swinging again. "That's true. But splitting up and trying it from two different angles isn't going to do anything, either. I'm moving to LA. I hate Cedar Grove, and I'm going home."

Clint shifted in his seat, moving forward, leaning elbows on knees—praying he could find the chink in Charles's newly reinforced armor.

He'd done it before.

Somehow, some way, he had to do it again.

"I wish you didn't feel that way, Charlie. I was hoping you'd begun to think of Cedar Grove as home. I had so many things planned for us to do—the 4-H thing, sledding and ice skating this winter. And for Christmas, I had a real special present planned."

Charles the Monetarist nearly turned at this, but caught himself. "Don't call me Charlie," he said. "You know I don't like it. And I don't need a present. I get lots of stuff from my dad."

"I'm sure you do," Clint said, feeling everything slipping. "Look, Charles, I'm going to level with you here. You're a smart kid and mature for your age and I'm just going to cut out the crap. Okay?"

Charles only shrugged, his small face hardening a fraction more.

"You mean a lot to me, Charles," Clint said, looking down at his hands. "A heck of a lot. I care what happens to you and I care if you're happy. So the thing is—"

"The thing is," Charles cut in, stone faced, "that you're here because you know my mom wants me back and you want to make *her* happy. Don't try to con me, Clinty. I know exactly what's going on."

"You don't know anything," Clint said, voice rising. "You don't know what your mother went through today, or what I went through, or what I'm still going through, for that matter! How do you think it feels to me to know I hurt you like this?"

"I'm not hurt," Charles said, but there was a light glimmer of tears in his eyes. "I just want to go home, and I decided to do it."

"Bull," Clint said. "You're hurt and I'm hurt and your mother's hurt. Everybody's hurt! And if we don't start talking and find a way to fix it, it's going to go on and on and—"

"There is no way to fix it!" Charles shouted, spinning to face him.

Then, realizing there was a staring crowd, he lowered his eyes. Tears spilled off his lashes, plopping on the lenses of his glasses.

"Come on," Clint said. "Let's go find some privacy."

"No," Charles said. "I'm not going anywhere with you and if you try to make me I'll tell them you're trying to kidnap me."

"*Kidnap* you?" Looking at him, Clint realized he would. He glanced around, suddenly nervous, just seeing himself landing in jail. Then his eyes narrowed. "Maybe I should," he said. "Maybe I should just haul you out of here, sit your tail on that chartered plane and have Jared fly us around in circles until you'll listen to me."

"You better not," Charles said. "I'll . . . what chartered plane?"

"The one I hired to get me here before you got to California and I wouldn't be able to talk to you."

"You chartered a plane?"

"I already said that. You're changing the subject. We're running out of time."

Plus he'd checked Candace's schedule and knew she'd be getting in soon. Right this minute he didn't really want to see her. Right this minute he had the feeling she wouldn't be thrilled to find him talking to her son. If she had wanted that, she probably wouldn't have objected to his going with her.

Clint closed his eyes. He hadn't thought that far ahead, only thought about Candace not wanting Charles to see them together. But maybe the truth was that after his actions this morning, she didn't want him dealing with Charles at all.

And maybe he shouldn't be, either.

He remembered thinking early on that the Whitneys and their problems were beyond his usual ken. He'd misguessed Charles's problems this morning and look where it had gotten them. In the middle of the Denver airport, everything as absolutely screwed up as it could possibly get.

"Listen," he said, his mouth going dry at the possibility that his good intentions might be making things worse. "Maybe I shouldn't have come. Maybe I should just do like you want and leave you alone."

He looked at the stony-faced child, suddenly doubting everything he'd ever thought he'd known.

"I think I'd better be going," he said. "Your mother's going to be getting in here shortly, and the more I think about it, the more I think I don't really want her to see me here. But the thing I came to say, Charles, is this. I care about you more than you could ever know. And I'm sorry about this morning. I didn't handle things right and I hurt you and I know that now and I'm sorry. And one more thing, kid. Whether you decide to live in California or Missouri or Timbuktu, I want you to get hold of this. If you ever need me for anything, I'm there."

He got up, checked his watch, knew he'd better get going. He'd messed things up sufficiently for one day, but he did feel better about having told Charles the truth. He also felt and hoped that when things settled down, Charles would feel better for this conversation, too.

"I guess I'd better go," he said, wishing the boy would look at him.

He wanted to hug him, but patted him on the shoulder instead, a shoulder that should have been soft and childlike, but that was hard with tension and pain instead.

"Goodbye, Charles," he said and heard the huskiness in his voice. Why couldn't he just go? Why had he come in the first place?

Because he'd had to try.

And now he had.

And he had failed.

He turned, feeling sick and beaten and exhausted. The long trek back to the Cessna seemed an impossible journey.

"Mom doesn't know you're here?" Charles asked, his clear voice carrying across the waiting room.

Clint turned. "No," he said, not caring who was watching, either.

"You came on your own?"

"Yes."

"And chartered a plane?"

"Yes."

"Why?"

The blue eyes blinked at him, and Clint saw in them his future—or at least, a very big part of what it could be. Baseball games and barbecues. Horseback rides and 4-H trophies. Fly fishing on Taggert's Stream.

"Because I love you," Clint said, and heard the murmurs of the other waiting passengers, but didn't care. "I love you and I wanted to try to fix things up between us. I didn't want to lose you, Charles. So I chartered a plane and followed you here."

Around them the other passengers fell silent, watching and waiting to see what would happen next.

Charles thought for a long minute, searching Clint's eyes for sincerity.

Then abruptly he hopped down from his chair and stood in front of it.

"Jeez, Clinty," he said, "you don't have to get so mushy. There's people around. They might think I'm your boyfriend or something."

Elated and mortified, Clint slapped his hands over his face and groaned. "Charlie," he said, "you're going to be the death of me yet."

For the first half of the trip from K.C. to Denver, Candace was sad—aching over the loss she knew she was going to have to create in their lives, regretting the pain the whole involvement had caused, anticipating the trials and stresses of starting over one more time in LA, and wondering how she could straighten out Charles alone.

He'd gone from bad to great to horrible over the five months since the move. Her only thought in her life had been to do what was best for him, and it had backfired royally.

She'd coddled and cajoled and bribed and gotten stern. She'd designed everything around what would or wouldn't make him happy. And in the end, he'd wound up running his own life, trying to run Clint's life, completely and ruthlessly running hers.

"This isn't about a horse show," Clint had said— was it only this morning? So much had happened, she hadn't, until now, had time to sit down and think.

But now, with the clouds around them and the miles melting away beneath, the past weeks, months, even years, ran through her mind.

And when had Charles seemed absolutely happiest, most proud of himself, most confident and serene?

During the past few months, since he'd known Clint.

Out at the Double C, Clint Blackwell was boss and made Charles and the older boys toe the line. He was firm but fair and when he talked, they listened. He'd taken five troubled boys, and by demanding their respect and letting them earn some on their own, he'd turned their lives around. In short months he'd taken four genuine delinquents and turned them into decent, hardworking, hard-playing, functional, churchgoing, team-playing boys. In short months he'd turned Charles into a regular kid. Well, almost.

But Charles was Charles, and Candace wouldn't have that any other way.

This isn't about a horse show. It's about letting a six-year-old run your life!

That child threatened me, Candace! He threatened me... ! I don't know what you've done to Charles! God, how irresponsible can you be?

You're giving him total control... making him into a tyrant! A child needs rules, boundaries. A six-year-old child is not *equipped to make the decisions in his life. You're the parent, Candace. You're not here to make him happy or to make him your friend. You have a job to do....*

And the more she thought about it as they cruised over Kansas, the more she knew he was right. She couldn't *make* Charles happy all the time. All she could do, and what she *owed* it to him to do, was to live her own life the best way she knew how, set the best example she could, demand some respect for herself and try to teach him the skills he would need to find his own happiness in this world.

If not, and if he continued to "con and manipulate," as one disgustingly wise rancher had put it, then the future for Charles was boundless indeed.

Yesterday, a temper tantrum. Today, blackmailing his father to arrange a cross-country trip. Tomorrow...who knew? But if she didn't take back the control she'd given up, Candace thought maybe the international banks should be given fair warning.

So for the rest of the trip, Candace didn't feel sad.

She felt mad.

And for the first time since the divorce, she felt confident of her own ability to raise her son. She would stop trying to be his friend and confidante and therapist, and start trying to be what he really needed her to be: his mother.

Confidence; yes, she could feel the liberating sensations growing inside her.

Confident.

And strong.

"Will you *really?*" Charles said, staring at Clint with huge blue eyes.

"I will." Clint nodded. "*If* things work out."

"They will," Charles said, all confidence as he chowed down on his second hot dog smothered with ketchup, cheese and relish.

They'd moved into the snack bar after making spectacles of themselves in the waiting area, neither of them regretting that they'd patched things up, but both feeling incredibly stupid by the time true confessions were all over.

Now they were both eating, kidding around—trying to be cool and pretend all the gushy, mushy junk never happened. They were two tough cowboys again, and Clint had to admit that the razzing, ribbing, joking kind of closeness they'd always had was a lot more comfortable for him.

But...the other things had needed to be said, and he'd done it and lived through it, and now things were better.

Now, he tried not to think about what Candace was going to do or think when she got here.

"They *will* work out," Charles said, grinning in a way that made Clint nervous.

"I hope so," Clint said. "You know how I feel about your mother, and I think she feels the same way about me."

"Oh, she does," Charles said. "And she'll say yes. I guarantee it."

"What does that mean?" Clint hated to ask.

When Candace's plane landed in Denver, she made a mad dash to check in for her connecting flight to LA.

Of course it was at the far end of the terminal, but right this minute she didn't mind. She felt energized and was actually glad to have the physical activity to burn off some of it. She wouldn't be in LA for hours yet, and she wanted some time to relax and calm and rehearse her plan of action.

Once she checked in, her plane wouldn't board for half an hour. She was hungry, she realized, striding along the carpeted corridor. She took note of a group of vending machines and then a regular snack bar. No time for real food. Maybe she'd...

Candace stopped so abruptly the skycap behind her rammed her with a cartload of luggage, almost knocking her down.

"I'm so sorry," the teenage boy said, rushing around his baggage to take her arm. "I didn't see you stop, and then—"

"It's okay," Candace mumbled, not hearing him anyway.

All she saw was a set of familiar heads huddled over hot dogs.

Stunned, she walked toward them.

"So the thing is, if she doesn't say yes, I'll just tell her I'm going to go live with Dad. She hates it when I say that and—"

"You certainly will *not* do that," Clint said. "Jeez, Charles, get a conscience."

"Huh?"

Clint shook his head. "Tell you what, whether I end up being your stepfather or not, you and I are gonna go round and round until you get this thing figured out. You can't go through life conning and blackmailing and throwing little baby tantrums when you don't get your way."

"But Mom's crazy about you. I'd only be getting her to do what she wants to do anyway."

"Charles..." He looked up over Charles's head and froze. Candace stood behind him, listening and looking like someone Charles might not want to mess with.

Before Clint could greet her, she put a finger to her lips, swearing him to secrecy.

"If it's what she wants anyway," Charles said, borderline pouting, "I don't see what's wrong with giving her a little ... nudge in the right direction."

Candace nodded, apparently deciding this was her cue.

"What's *wrong* with that, Charles Whitney..." she said, and Charles, startled, leapt out of his seat.

"Mom!"

"Yes, Mom," Candace said. "What's wrong with your little plan is that it is *not* up to you to decide what I want and don't want—*or* what I can and can't do."

"But, Mom—"

"Hush," Candace said. "I'll talk, you listen. Things are going to change around our house, Charles. Things have gotten completely out of hand, and we are going to turn them around. Now this little stunt you pulled today was the last straw. By the time we get home, I'm going to have a whole page full of restrictions that you *will* honor—or else."

"Or else what?"

Candace bent down to hold his gaze at eye level—and show him that she meant it. "Or else you'll be in deeper trouble than you ever imagined."

Charles wanted to challenge this, Clint could tell. He wanted to get examples, scenarios, grounds for rebuttal, but Candace never flinched under his wise little stare.

Clint was so proud of her he wanted to stand up and applaud. Only thing was, he wasn't sure she wouldn't tell him a thing or three, too.

Finally Charles lost his defiant look and sighed. "Okay. I guess today was pretty rotten."

"You bet it was," Candace said, then her face softened, too. "And you *are* in trouble. But boy am I glad to see you're also okay."

Then he grinned sheepishly and Candace hugged him. Over his head, she looked at Clint—and frowned.

"What are you doing here, anyway?"

"He chartered a plane," Charles piped up, disentangling himself and pushing up his glasses.

"He did?" Candace said, then looked at Clint. "You did? Why?"

"To head me off at the pass," Charles said, and Clint shrugged, letting Charles tell the story. "He thought you might be mad that he came all the way out here to talk to me, but I told him you wouldn't— are you?"

"I . . . I don't know. I don't even know what's going on. You *chartered* a *plane?*"

Clint thought it was time to explain himself. "The thing is, I didn't want Charles to get away for too long before I had a chance to try to patch things up between us. So I got a friend of mine to fly me up so I could see Charlie here before he moved his little self to California."

"I see," Candace said, then surveyed the junk food remains on the table. "And I take it you succeeded in . . . patching things up?"

Clint shrugged, looked unconcerned. "Yeah, I guess so. What do you think, Charlie?"

Charles shrugged. "I guess. Yeah, I'd say we're all right, Clinty."

Candace rolled her eyes. "I swear, between the two of you . . ."

"The *three* of us," Charles said.

"What?" Candace frowned.

"Among the *three* of us. From now on, that's the way me and Clinty think it ought to be."

"You do," Candace said, wondering what the heck Clint had done with Charles in the little time he could have been here.

Gotten through, a little voice said. *Once again, Clint had managed to get through.*

Would this man be good in her son's life?

Candace was ashamed to have even asked the question.

And while there were never any guarantees, Clint's love for Charles was more than evident. In this life, that was as good a guarantee for the future as you could get.

"Yeah," Charles said. "We do. And guess what. After you and Clint get married, he's going to change the name of the Double C to the *Triple* C! Isn't that rad? I've never had a ranch named after me."

"Uh, Charles," Clint said, looking uncomfortable, "that's like I told you. It's something I'd want to do *if*. Remember I told you *if?*"

"If you get married?" Charles said, all false innocence.

"No," Clint said, turning to Candace, taking her hand. "*If,* after your mother has a chance to think about it, she says yes."

"What's to think about?" Charles said. "Go on, Mom, tell him. I mean, the guy's going to name a *ranch* after you! Go on, Mom, go ahead and tell him."

"Charles," Candace said evenly, not looking at her son. "Just *shut* up."

Charles did.

Candace took one long look into Clint Blackwell's gray eyes.

"Yes," she said.

Charles whooped in delight.

And the other patrons of the airport snack bar applauded.

* * * * *

HE'S MORE THAN
A MAN, HE'S
ONE OF OUR

ONE MAN'S VOW
Diana Whitney

Single father Judd Tanner had his hands full with a houseful of
boys and one orphaned goddaughter. But a woman's touch
was the last thing he wanted. Women, he knew, were experts
at one thing—leaving. It didn't matter to Judd that from the
moment she'd arrived, Leslie Leighton McVay had his boys
behaving and his godchild smiling. It would take more than
that to convince him that the pretty drifter was really home
to stay....

Find out just what it takes for Judd to love again, in
Diana Whitney's ONE MAN'S VOW, available in June.

Fall in love with our **Fabulous Fathers**—and join the
Silhouette Romance family!

FF693

Silhouette
R O M A N C E™

Silhouette Romance celebrates June brides and grooms and *You're Invited!* Be our guest as five special couples find the magic ingredients for happily-*wed*-ever-afters! Look for these wonderful stories by some of your favorite authors...

WED

R O M A N C E™

Is your father a Fabulous Father?

Then enter him in Silhouette Romance's

"FATHER OF THE YEAR" Contest
and you can both win some great prizes! Look for contest details
in the FABULOUS FATHER titles available in June, July
and August...

ONE MAN'S VOW by Diana Whitney
Available in June

ACCIDENTAL DAD by Anne Peters
Available in July

INSTANT FATHER by Lucy Gordon
Available in August

Only from

Silhouette
R O M A N C E™

SMYTHESHIRE, MASSACHUSETTS.

Small town. Big secrets.

Silhouette Romance invites you to visit Elizabeth August's intriguing small town, a place with an unusual legacy rooted deep in the past....

THE VIRGIN WIFE (#921) February 1993
HAUNTED HUSBAND (#922) March 1993
LUCKY PENNY (#945) June 1993
A WEDDING FOR EMILY (#953) August 1993

Elizabeth August's SMYTHESHIRE, MASSACHUSETTS—
This sleepy little town has plenty to keep you up at night.
Only from Silhouette Romance!

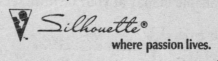

A romantic collection that
will touch your heart....

to
Mother
with
Love
'93

Diana Palmer
Debbie Macomber
Judith Duncan

As part of your annual tribute to
motherhood, join three of Silhouette's
best-loved authors as they celebrate the
joy of one of our most precious gifts—
mothers.

Available in May at your favorite retail outlet.

Only from 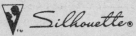 *Silhouette*®

—where passion lives.